"I'm all Caden's got."

"You've got your family to support you."

"Yes, but—" Panic reared and bucked in Seth's chest. "Luke and Tracy left me the Hollister ranch, as well. It's Caden's legacy. But I don't know the first thing about running a cattle business. I can't *do* this. I can't be Caden's daddy. I don't know how."

"Stand up," Rachel said, moving to his side. Her voice was strong and determined. "Now, take the baby in your arms."

Seth swallowed hard but tucked a sleeping Caden against his shoulder. The boy seemed to curve right into Seth. The gentle rhythm of the child's breath against his neck somehow soothed Seth.

"What are you feeling?" Rachel asked gently.

How *did* he feel?

Nervous. Overwhelmed. Panicked. Devastated. And yet, there was something more hovering just below the surface.

He was responsible for this little human being. And even though it meant his entire life had just been turned upside down and backward, there was something somehow…*right* about holding Caden in his arms.

Award-winning author **Deb Kastner** writes stories of faith, family and community in a small-town Western setting. Deb's books contain sigh-worthy heroes and strong heroines facing obstacles that draw them closer to each other and the Lord. She lives in Colorado with her husband and is blessed with three daughters and two grandchildren. She enjoys spoiling her grandkids, movies, music (The Texas Tenors!), singing in the church choir and exploring Colorado on horseback.

Books by Deb Kastner

Love Inspired

Cowboy Country

Yuletide Baby
The Cowboy's Forever Family
The Cowboy's Surprise Baby
The Cowboy's Twins
Mistletoe Daddy
The Cowboy's Baby Blessing

Lone Star Cowboy League: Boys Ranch

The Doctor's Texas Baby

Lone Star Cowboy League

A Daddy for Her Triplets

Email Order Brides

Phoebe's Groom
The Doctor's Secret Son
The Nanny's Twin Blessings
Meeting Mr. Right

Visit the Author Profile page at Harlequin.com for more titles.

The Cowboy's Baby Blessing

Deb Kastner

HARLEQUIN® LOVE INSPIRED®

If you purchased this book without a cover you should be aware that this book is stolen property. It was reported as "unsold and destroyed" to the publisher, and neither the author nor the publisher has received any payment for this "stripped book."

LOVE INSPIRED BOOKS

Recycling programs for this product may not exist in your area.

ISBN-13: 978-0-373-62285-6

The Cowboy's Baby Blessing

Copyright © 2017 by Debra Kastner

All rights reserved. Except for use in any review, the reproduction or utilization of this work in whole or in part in any form by any electronic, mechanical or other means, now known or hereinafter invented, including xerography, photocopying and recording, or in any information storage or retrieval system, is forbidden without the written permission of the editorial office, Love Inspired Books, 195 Broadway, New York, NY 10007 U.S.A.

This is a work of fiction. Names, characters, places and incidents are either the product of the author's imagination or are used fictitiously, and any resemblance to actual persons, living or dead, business establishments, events or locales is entirely coincidental.

This edition published by arrangement with Love Inspired Books.

® and TM are trademarks of Love Inspired Books, used under license. Trademarks indicated with ® are registered in the United States Patent and Trademark Office, the Canadian Intellectual Property Office and in other countries.

www.Harlequin.com

Printed in U.S.A.

The Lord is near to all who call upon Him,
To all who call upon Him in truth.
—*Psalms* 145:18

To my forever sweetheart, Joe.
We've been through a lot, you and I,
and I wouldn't trade any of it for the world.
Every day with you is a great joy,
and I'm so blessed by our thirty years together.
Here's to thirty more.

Chapter One

Rachel Perez was looking for a man, not a monkey.

And she was most definitely *not* looking for a date, unlike many of the other single ladies scattered across the lawn at the First Annual Bachelors and Baskets Auction in Serendipity, Texas. What better way to nab themselves a bachelor for romantic reasons than a bachelor auction?

But that was *so* not Rachel.

No, not even close.

Rachel was in the market for a guy who was handy at fixing things—and she needed him, like, yesterday. She needed someone to tear down the well-used play set in her backyard and replace it with something new and to government specifications. The recertification status of the day care she ran out of her home depended on picking the right man for the job.

That was why she was glad that her town had chosen this particular type of "bachelor" auction to raise funds to build a senior center for the town—an auction that wasn't actually about getting dates with bachelors at all.

The Bachelors and Baskets Auction had started out

with the idea of hosting only true bachelors, but because the auction was for such an important cause, married men had jumped on the bandwagon, as well. Every man had his own unique skill set to offer to the crowd.

Making the auction a full-town event had also opened the bidding to a wider range of individuals. Single and married women alike were encouraged to bid on the men of their choice to help them with whatever projects needed doing around their homes and ranches.

Rachel suspected there would be a lot of husbands washing dishes and folding many loads of laundry before this day was done.

And determined not to be outdone by the men, the ladies in Serendipity had soon added their own contributions to the auction—loaded picnic baskets as a prize for the fellows they won. Virtually everyone in town was involved at some level. That was just the way the folks in Serendipity were—generous to a fault and ready with any excuse to get together and have a celebration. And willing to buckle down and put in good work, too, when it was needed. Surely there'd be someone perfect for the job of fixing up her outdoor play area for the kids in her care.

She intended to be picky about her choice. Someone older with lots of experience.

Even so, she had to admit she was amused by former army corporal Seth Howell's grand entrance. He might be too young and flighty to fulfill her requirements, but he was admittedly fun to watch.

At a full run, Seth banked his feet off one tree trunk before swinging from the branches of another. He hurdled over a bench and backflipped onto the platform where the auction was being held.

Jo Spencer, the redheaded owner of Cup O' Jo's Café, second mother to most of the town, as well as self-appointed auctioneer of this event, cackled with delight at his antics. She put a hammer in his grasp so he could continue to entertain the audience by displaying his abilities and showmanship.

He swung it around in circles and jabbed it a couple of times like a rapier, then posed like a well-built statue of a carpenter, showing off the sinews of his muscular biceps. Seth was shorter and leaner than some of the other cowboys Rachel had seen auctioned off so far—like the gigantic McKenna brothers, who towered over most of the crowd, but Seth was clearly in prime shape.

"Now, you can see for yourself, folks, what a unique specimen we have right here," Jo began. "He is ready and willing to help you with whatever odd jobs you've got planned for him, and you can be certain he will be adding his own brand of fun to the mix.

"Doesn't that sound lovely? Now, don't be deceived by his incredible physical prowess. Seth is not just a good-looking hunk of a man—he has a brain, to boot. You may not know this, but Seth is the fellow who single-handedly designed and built the new playground in the park. The man has *skillzzz*."

"Jo's right." Lizzie Emerson, Rachel's best friend, elbowed her in the ribs and grinned like she'd just pulled off a major prank. "That guy is cute *and* talented. And he couldn't be more perfect. He made the play set at the park. You need a play set built. He can do that—and so much more. Maybe one of your *odd jobs* could be for him to take you out for dinner."

Rachel locked gazes with her sixteen-year-old daughter, Zooey, and rolled her eyes. "For someone else, maybe, but I'm not looking for a date. You know perfectly well that all I'm looking for is a handyman to help bring my day care up to snuff before the next inspection. I don't have time for a romantic relationship even if I wanted one. Which I don't," she added when Lizzie's eyes glowed with mischief. "Even if I was looking for a date, I wouldn't try to find him at a bachelor auction. No—he's not the one for me."

Which was too bad, really. With what she now knew of Seth's background, she might have considered bidding on him, even if she had to put up with an occasional goofy antic. She'd seen the amazing wood-and-pipe structures he'd built for the kids in the park. She could easily imagine a similar structure gracing her backyard and replacing the well-worn swing set and climbing tower she now possessed.

But thanks to Lizzie and Zooey, bidding on Seth was out of the question, with the pressure she'd be under to make her work with him some kind of romantic rendezvous. The new playground in the park was nice, but under the circumstances, it was not enough to tempt her to make an offer on him.

Too much trouble, with a capital *T*.

"Which one of you pretty ladies is going to open the bidding on this handsome fellow?" Jo called, looking out into the audience. "Grab those pocketbooks and bid as generously as you can. Our senior center is just awaitin' to be built with the money we raise here today, and Seth's worth every dime you spend, don't you think?"

Zooey laughed and snatched the three crisp one-hundred-dollar bills Rachel had tucked in her hand, waving one of them in the air so Jo would see.

"One hundred dollars!"

"*What* do you think you are doing?" Rachel snapped, enunciating every word as she frantically reached for her daughter's wrist.

Zooey danced away, laughing in delight.

Lizzie offered a complicit grin. "We are buying you a bachelor. Which you desperately need, by the way. You need a *man* in your life, at least as much as you need a handyman. We know it, and so do you, if you're being honest with yourself."

"Oh, for crying out loud, you two. Didn't you listen to what I just said?" She was relieved when elsewhere on the lawn someone bumped the bid up to $125.

"Seth is the best of both worlds," Zooey pointed out. "You aren't going to find a better handyman out there when it comes to building playhouses."

Her statement might be valid, but Rachel wasn't about to concede. Not since the whole *both worlds* thing came into play with them. Dealing with a pair of matchmakers could lead only to embarrassment, for her and for Seth. She needed to nip this in the bud, right now. She scurried to make a mental list of reasons Seth wouldn't work out for her.

She wasn't coming up with much.

"I don't want—" she started to say, but her daughter interrupted her.

"Seth will be good for you, and he's the exact right fit for repairing your play equipment at the day care. No more arguments."

At the moment Rachel couldn't think of any, other than that Zooey's idea of the perfect candidate and hers were as different as night from day. As with so many things lately, this was just going to have to be another topic on which they couldn't seem to see eye to eye.

"One fifty for Seth!" Zooey shouted, squealing in delight when Jo pointed to her and acknowledged her bid.

"Zooey Maria Josephina Perez. Stop bidding and give me back my money this instant."

"I always know I'm in trouble when my mom uses my full name," she told Lizzie. "I think that's how she decided what my name would be when I was born."

"Zooey Maria Josephina Perez, get out of that tree before you fall and break your neck!" Zooey quipped.

Rachel sighed inwardly. If only it were that simple. Raising a teenager was much more difficult than having a good name to scold them with. For the scolding to work, the teenager first needed to be willing to listen to what the mother had to say.

Zooey's words were meant as a joke, but Rachel's heart tightened just a little. She loved seeing Zooey happy and carefree as she was acting today, focused on something that she genuinely seemed to believe would make her mother happy, but lately that had been the exception to the rule. It wasn't even funny to *jest* about Zooey getting into trouble—not when it was happening in fact, and all too often lately. And though they'd always been close, nothing Rachel said to her daughter seemed to get through to her at all anymore.

"It's for a good cause," Lizzie reminded Rachel, redirecting her attention to the stage.

"Yes, of course it is. To raise funds to build the senior center. I'm aware of that, as is everyone else who has come out today."

"No," Lizzie replied tartly. "The senior center is important, of course, but I was referring to finding you a single guy who is as good for your social life as he is for your day care. It could happen."

Rachel opened her mouth to protest once again, but Lizzie held up her hands to stop her.

"You heard Jo. Seth built the new playground in the park. You're looking for a man to spiff up your playhouse and swing set. Face it, girl. Seth Howell is exactly the man you need for the job. That he's nice on the eyes is purely going to be a side benefit."

Maybe he was the best man for the playhouse job, and he was rather handsome, but Rachel wasn't going to dig herself any deeper by admitting she privately agreed with her friend.

The guy was good-looking. If he was hoping to get a date out of this, he deserved to have that chance—but not with her. She would not embarrass Seth by being the high bidder when clearly there were any number of pretty young ladies spread out over the green seeking his undivided attention in far more interesting ways than anything she could offer.

She was confident he wouldn't want to be stuck with a woman who had long since exited the dating scene and who had nothing more on her mind than getting her play equipment recertification-ready.

The bidding war on Seth, who had passed the hammer back to Jo and was currently amusing the crowd by walking on his hands, was inching up in twenty-five-dollar increments. Her daughter had, thankfully, stopped participating in the back-and-forth volley, letting the younger women who *really* wanted social time with Seth fight it out between them. Rachel had brought her hard-earned cash with the intent to bid on one of Serendipity's best handymen or weekend do-it-yourselfers, most of whom were old or married or both, and she was fine with that. Better than fine—even if none of them had been the one who'd built the playground in the park. She *definitely* didn't care that none of them could hold a candle to Seth's youthful good looks, even an upside-down Seth whose blood was rushing to his face.

When the bidding finally passed the $300 mark, the knots in Rachel's shoulders relaxed. He was officially out of her budget now, so there'd be no more nonsense about Seth Howell. She would wait and bid on another man who would be willing and able help her spiff up her day care without putting crazy romantic ideas into her daughter's and best friend's heads.

Now that she was legitimately out of the running for Seth, she was beginning to enjoy watching the excitement the young, eager women were currently bringing to the auction. It was kind of cute, actually, seeing the hope and excitement in their expressions as they bid.

Eventually, the bidding stalled at $375. A happy seventy-five dollars more than Rachel could afford, thankfully.

"Going once," Jo announced. She bobbed her head so her red curls bounced and hovered her gavel over the makeshift podium. "Going twice."

Jo paused, her gaze spanning the green. She had just raised her gavel for the crack of a sale when Zooey spoke up.

"Four hundred," she announced brightly.

"Wait, what?" Rachel said aloud.

Zooey knew perfectly well how hard Rachel had had to scrape the bottom of the barrel for the $300 she'd collected to bid, and even then only because the need for a senior center was so great and because she could justify the remodeling work as a business expense.

And now she was going to be out another hundred? She didn't want to be stingy when the money was going to such a good cause, but she was on a tight budget.

Her home day care kept a roof over her and Zooey's heads and food on the table, but there wasn't a lot of wiggle room for extras—like bidding on a goofy young man doing flips and handstands just because he was *cute*.

"Sold, to—" Jo paused as Zooey pointed both hands toward Rachel "—Rachel Perez."

Even with everyone's eyes on her, Rachel balked for a moment and then caught her daughter's elbow. "That hundred dollars is going to come out of your allowance."

Thankfully, Rachel had enough spare cash in her wallet to cover the difference, but that wasn't the point. Her daughter had taken her decision right out of her hands.

"I know it will," Zooey agreed cheerfully. She reached into the pocket of her blue jeans and withdrew a wad of five crumpled twenty-dollar bills. "Don't worry. I've got it covered. I've been saving up. You don't even need to worry about paying me back. Now take the money and go up there and rope yourself a Cowboy Charming."

Rachel momentarily considered withdrawing the bid, but she didn't want to humiliate herself—or Seth—in a public venue.

How would it look if she backed out now? Would everyone think she was too flighty to know her own mind? Or that she didn't think Seth was good enough?

At least he had the *skillzzz*, as Jo had phrased it, to repair the playground equipment for the day care, which, at the end of the day, was all that really mattered.

She could deal. She *would* deal.

She huffed and snatched the money from her daughter's grasp, then threaded her way through the crowd to the staging area. She was well aware of what she would be required to do as the winning bidder and her face flushed with heat as she handed off the cash in exchange for a lariat.

Lovely. Now all she had to do to get this over and done with was make a public spectacle of herself, thanks to her incorrigible daughter and her best friend. She supposed she would have ended up on the platform being required to throw a lasso to "rope" the man she'd won either way, but she doubted that with all the silly antics Seth had demonstrated, he would make this easy for her.

Not to mention the fact that she'd never thrown a rope before. Despite that she lived square in the middle of the country, she'd never even visited a ranch or ridden a horse, much less roped a cow.

How was she supposed to lasso a guy who couldn't stand still for more than one second at a time?

Yeah, that was *so* not going to happen.

Seth's bright blue eyes met hers, full of impetuousness and humor. It took her aback for a moment. She'd forgotten what it felt like to be that lighthearted and carefree.

Maybe she'd never been.

"You've got this," Seth assured her, gesturing for her to throw the rope. Despite his grandstanding before, he was ignoring the audience now to smile supportively at her—a purely kind gesture that left her feeling a bit flustered.

"I wouldn't be so sure about that."

Seth's smile turned into a toothy grin. "Why don't you toss that thing and we'll see?"

Good grief. It was probably better for her to throw the rope and be done with it. She had no idea what she was supposed to do when she missed, because up until this point in the auction, all the men had been successfully roped, one way or another. Sometimes the cowboys had to be artful in getting that rope around them, but so far every single one of them had managed.

Rachel was bound to disappoint everyone with her pathetic attempt at lassoing Seth. Hopefully, the crowd would just let her retreat gracefully off the stage with her "prize" when she failed.

Releasing her breath on a sigh, she aimed the loop like a Frisbee and threw her lariat in Seth's general direction.

As she knew it would, it didn't even come close to flying over his head.

More like waist high.

How humiliating.

But before she could so much as blink, Seth dived forward, over and into the lariat, rather than under it. She gasped in surprise as he tucked his body and somersaulted to his feet, the lariat successfully tightened around his waist.

He offered his hand and gestured toward the platform stairs with another cheeky grin.

"Ready for lunch?"

Rachel couldn't find her voice, so she merely nodded as the crowd applauded them both.

Great. Her first thought of Seth being half man, half monkey was apparently not that far off the mark.

He might be well able to come to her rescue where

repairing the playhouse was concerned, but she had major doubts about how easy he would be to work with. He seemed like a nice enough man, but he didn't appear to take anything too seriously.

Would he go off swinging through the trees when he was supposed to be building playground equipment?

She glanced over to Zooey and Lizzie, expecting to see smug looks on their faces, but they'd already lost interest in her and now stood with their heads together, no doubt debating the pros and cons of the next bachelor on the docket. Lizzie hadn't put in her bid yet—and she *was* looking for a bachelor, someone she could eventually call her sweetheart.

Rachel considered rejoining them and then discarded the idea. Her impish daughter and equally mischievous best friend were bound to embarrass her—and worse, Seth—and she'd just as soon wait as long as possible before that eventuality.

Besides, Seth was probably hungry from all that backflipping and handstanding he'd done. At least if she had Seth to herself, she would be able to find out when and how she could avail him of his talents—those of the non-branch-swinging variety.

She led him across the community green to where she'd left her picnic basket under the cool shade of an old oak tree. She'd had the toddlers in her day care decorate the basket as part of arts-and-crafts time. It was now threaded with multicolored ribbons and randomly dotted with finger paint. Rachel was proud of the creation, and especially of her kids.

"Your basket looks awesome," Seth complimented.

She turned and met his gaze, half expecting to find

mockery in his eyes, but he was totally earnest, insofar as she could tell. His smile looked sincere.

"Thank you. My day-care kids made it for me."

"I can tell it was created with love," he said, sinking down onto the checked wool blanket she'd spread on the ground before him.

She smiled, pleased by his thoughtfulness. He was clearly a nice guy. Maybe this experience wouldn't be a total disaster after all. She smiled appreciatively and laid out the classic country picnic fare of fried chicken, macaroni salad and baked beans, with chocolate cupcakes for dessert.

Seth opened the water she offered him and downed the entire bottle without taking a breath. Wordlessly, she handed him a second bottle.

"Thirsty much?" she asked when he took another long drink.

He grinned. "Just rehydrating. Wait until you see my appetite."

She gestured to the food. "It's all yours."

Although technically, it wasn't. She couldn't forget that Zooey would be around before long with her own healthy appetite. Rachel had packed some of Zooey's favorites.

In preparation, Rachel fixed her daughter a plate and set it aside, then filled a plate for herself.

"Eating for two?" he teased.

For the briefest moment Seth's words took on an ugly context, one she'd long ago fought and overcome. She wasn't reed thin like Lizzie and even Zooey, and she accepted now that she never would be.

As a child, she'd been bullied. Worse than that, even, when she'd become a teenager.

But the glimmer in Seth's eyes wasn't cruel. He was joshing her about the two plates she'd fixed. She wasn't going to make it a sore point just because at one time in her life she'd had low self-esteem because of her weight.

She laughed and casually leaned back on her palms, crossing her feet at the ankles.

"This extra one is for my daughter, Zooey. She's still following the auction, helping my best friend, Lizzie, pick out the perfect handsome bachelor for a date, but I imagine she'll be around as soon as she gets hungry."

"Was that your daughter I saw bidding on your behalf?"

Rachel nodded and shifted her gaze away from him, suddenly uncomfortable and embarrassed that he'd noticed that she hadn't been doing her own bidding. She also worried that he might have misconstrued her words.

If Lizzie was looking for a handsome bachelor to date, it stood to reason that Rachel had been looking for the same exact thing. And that Seth might think that bachelor was him.

Oh dear.

"Yes, that's Zooey," she cut in quickly, before he had too much time to think about what she'd said previously. "She's sixteen. To be perfectly honest with you, she had an entirely different idea than me on what I was looking for. She took over my bidding completely without my consent." Suddenly realizing how insulting that might sound, she scrambled to backpedal. "I didn't— That is— I wouldn't—"

When she stammered to a halt and heat rushed to her face, he finished her sentence for her.

"You wouldn't have chosen to bid on me."

***

No big deal, he told himself, but knowing that Rachel hadn't really wanted to win him still pricked at his pride.

Rachel met his gaze, her deep brown eyes thoughtful and expressive.

"No. To be honest, I probably wouldn't have. That is, originally, I *would* have considered you, especially regarding the particular tasks I have in mind for you to do for me." She took a great gulp of air. "But then Lizzie and my daughter got it in their minds to—"

She stammered to a halt. Inhaled another ragged breath. Exhaled on a deep sigh. Seth wanted to say something to make her feel better, but he honestly had no clue what he could offer. Frankly, it was strange to him to see her this flustered. He knew her only in passing, but she'd always given off this air of calm competence that he admired, seeming sure of herself in every situation.

Well, apparently not this one.

"I'm afraid all I will be able to offer you is some general fix-it work on the play yard of my in-home day care," she said at last.

He took a sip of cold water and gestured with his hand. "As opposed to…?"

Her cheeks, which were already flushed a pretty pink, now turned bright red, and she broke her gaze away from his.

"Okay," she muttered under her breath. "I'm just going to say it."

She paused dramatically. "As opposed to a date. I feel like I cheated you out of something special. You know, something more, er, romantic. You would have been better off with one of the beautiful younger ladies who were bidding on you for your—" her voice tightened and she squinted as she choked out the last part of her sentence "—good looks."

He sat up straighter as his wilted ego reinflated faster than a balloon on a helium pump.

"No worries on that front," he assured her with a grin. "I'm glad you won the bid on me. Relieved, even. You just saved me from what could have been an awkward situation. I assure you I'm not looking for a girlfriend, not even a casual one. That wouldn't be fair to her. I'm only home for a few weeks before I'm heading off to college."

"That's exciting. I never made it to college. Have you picked a school yet?"

"Texas State University. I'm a little nervous about it," he admitted. "I've never been a great student, and it's not like I'm right out of high school, so I'll probably stick out like a sore thumb."

"Oh, I wouldn't worry too much about that. It's not like you're over-the-hill, and many adults these days are choosing to go back to school after they've been out in the real world for a while."

A brief cloud of sadness crossed over his heart. "That, I've done. Seen the real world, I mean, in the army. I'm looking forward to putting my full focus on my academics."

And keep his mind off everything he'd experienced while on tour. He was haunted by questions and guilt that wouldn't leave him alone. He was hoping he'd be so busy studying that he wouldn't have time for reflection on just how cruel he'd seen the "real world" be.

It couldn't get much more real than watching his

best friend, Luke, being gunned down right in front of him, hit by a sniper who barely missed Seth, but that wasn't something he wanted to share with a woman he'd barely met.

He didn't even like to think about it, much less talk about it.

"I'm so sorry. I know you were in the army. I didn't mean to remind you of hard times."

He shrugged. "Life is what it is. I've learned that I have to accept it and move forward. The key is to watch my attitude. I've chosen to remain positive."

"That's a wonderful outlook, and one I try to follow myself, although I'm not always successful at it. Sometimes it's easier to see the glass as half-empty."

Her gaze dropped and she blew out a breath. He waited for her to finish her thought, but she remained quiet. He knew what she wanted to say but couldn't.

Easier, but not better.

"I'm majoring in athletic training," he said to fill the silence.

"Based on your demonstration before, I'd say that ought to be right up your alley." She snapped back to the present and smiled at him, although he could see it was forced. "What do you plan to do when you graduate? Coach high school sports?"

He shrugged. He wasn't much of a planner and never had been. He only vaguely pictured his future beyond the challenge of four years of hitting the books. He knew from experience that too much could change between now and then. What was the point of making all these grandiose plans only to discover life is nothing like you expect it to be?

"I don't know yet. I think it'd be cool to work with

a pro sports team. Football or baseball, maybe, or even basketball. That'd give me the opportunity to travel the country, which I'd like to do. Or if not that, then maybe I could work with a college sports program. I'd like to think I could make a difference with the kids coming through the ranks."

"I suspect you'd be very good at that, given the *skillzzz* I saw you display today."

He laughed at her exact replication of Jo's word, all the way down to the crackly tone of voice that the old redhead had used.

"I'm probably just kidding myself thinking I can get into the big leagues, but I figure I might as well reach for the sky, right?"

"Or swing for it." She laughed. "What's that called, anyway? That thing you were doing earlier with the swinging and jumping and backflips?"

His smile widened. "Parkour. It's basically focusing your mind with the intent of seeing and interacting with your environment in a different way. It puts everything into perspective. You should try it sometime. I could give you a lesson or two."

Her eyes widened in surprise and then she burst out laughing.

"With this body?" She gestured at herself from head to toe. "I don't think so."

He didn't see anything wrong with her body. She was full figured, but in a healthy way. Besides, parkour was a mental exercise as much as a physical one.

"You shouldn't limit yourself, Rachel. Parkour isn't about what you can't do—it's about what you *can*."

"I believe I'll stick to working out in my living room to my exercise dance DVDs, thank you very much.

Somewhere no one can see how awkward I look when I move."

He wanted to press her but sensed this wasn't the time. Plus, this was the first time he'd really spoken to her—brief chitchat at church or his family's grocery store didn't count—and he didn't want to give her the wrong impression about parkour. Or about *him*.

"What about your daughter? Do you think she might enjoy parkour?"

Rachel voraciously shook her head, her dark hair flipping over one shoulder.

"Oh, no. She needs to concentrate on her academics right now if she's going to get into a good college. She didn't pass two of her classes last year and consequently is in summer school right now. It's not that she's not smart," she modified. "She just hasn't been applying herself lately. I'm trying to encourage her to do better in summer school. Anyway, sports aren't really Zooey's thing."

"Did I hear my name?" Seth's gaze shifted to the teenager who'd jogged up to Rachel. Zooey was a pretty, dark-haired, dark-eyed teenager who looked a lot like her mother. The girl dropped onto her knees next to the picnic basket and flashed a friendly smile at Seth.

"I was telling Seth here what a pickle you are, taking over the bidding on my behalf."

Zooey stuck out her tongue at Rachel and reached for the plate Rachel handed her. "Someone had to do it. You don't mind, do you, Seth?"

He chuckled. "No, of course not. In fact, I'm thinking this day turned out rather well."

"Ha. Told you, Mom." She picked up a chicken drumstick, took a bite and pointed it toward Seth.

"Have you tried your chicken yet? My mom makes the best fried chicken ever."

"Don't talk with your mouth full," Rachel admonished. "And we haven't said grace yet."

Seth had been reaching for his chicken breast, but he stopped midmovement at Rachel's reminder that they needed to pray before their meal.

It wasn't something he was used to doing—not since his youth when he lived with his parents. He was used to diving straight into his meal, and this meal definitely seemed worth diving into. His stomach growled when the delectable, greasy smell of fried chicken reached his nose, and his mouth watered in anticipation. He usually limited himself to grilled meat served with lots of fresh fruits and vegetables, but he wasn't about to pass up homemade fried chicken.

This was a special occasion, right?

It was all he could do not to take a bite of his chicken, but he restrained himself and politely bowed his head.

"Would you like to say grace?"

With his eyes closed, he didn't immediately realize Rachel was speaking to him.

"Seth?"

His eyes popped open to find Rachel and Zooey both staring at him.

"I—er—I'm more of a Christmas and Easter kind of man. So I— Well, I'm out of practice. You go ahead." His voice sounded stilted and awkward, even to him.

"I'm sorry. I just assumed— I see your parents and sister at church every Sunday. I didn't mean to make you feel uncomfortable."

"You didn't," he assured her, even though he was itching in his skin.

He searched his mind for a way to describe his current relationship with the Lord, but nothing sounded right. It was too complicated for casual conversation. He believed in God, but God hadn't always been there for him.

Certainly not lately. Not when it really counted.

He was relieved when she spoke, removing the need for a coherent explanation.

"Let's thank the Lord for our food."

Quietly and with gentle reverence, she offered heartfelt gratitude for the food, the day and the company.

Seth shifted uncomfortably. He'd been raised in a Christian home and, since he'd returned from the army, occasionally attended church services with his family, but religion didn't play a big part in his life anymore.

He cracked his eyes open to watch Rachel pray and noticed he wasn't the only one feeling uncomfortable. Zooey's eyes were also open, her gaze on her folded hands. Or rather, she was frowning at her clenched hands. He was surprised she didn't seem tapped into faith. He certainly had been at her age, with his family's example all around him, and from the way that Rachel prayed, it was clear that faith was important to her and played a big role in her home.

Rachel's grace wasn't dry or bottled, but rather she spoke from her heart, which Seth admired and, if he was being honest, envied. He missed the innocence of his youth, of a faith that transcended the trials of daily life, but he'd seen far too much of the world not to question what he believed.

Still, he echoed her *amen*.

Zooey scooped a forkful of macaroni salad into her mouth and chewed slowly. A group of young men Seth guessed to be around Zooey's age walked by, jostling and shoving and trying to talk over each other. Zooey didn't turn her head, but her gaze trailed after the guys.

Rachel must have seen that, as well.

"It's a good thing they didn't allow the teenage guys to participate in the auction," she said after swallowing her bite of baked beans.

The boys had moved out of hearing distance, but that didn't stop the blush that rose to the teenager's cheeks.

"Mom," she whispered harshly. "That is so uncool. They could have heard you."

A little adolescent and overdramatic for Seth's taste, but it was an amusing scene, at least until Zooey tossed down her plate and popped to her feet.

"I am *so* out of here."

"Sit down and finish eating." Rachel's voice was low and even, but Seth could hear the barely contained tension coating her voice. Her daughter seemed all too willing to ignore it.

"Zooey," Rachel called after her, but the teenager loped away as if she hadn't heard, joining a group of friends on the other side of the green.

Rachel sighed and rested her forehead against her palm. "I'm getting a migraine. Sometimes I really don't know what to do with that girl."

Seth chuckled. "She's a teenager. Most of the time, rebellion is written in their DNA. Are you going to tell me you didn't get into a few scrapes and give your mom a hassle when you were sixteen?"

She scoffed. "I had a newborn baby when I was sixteen. My mother didn't care for the idea of becoming a grandmother at such a young age and she threw me out of the house."

Seth's gut tightened. "Are you serious?"

"Unfortunately, yes. My mom and dad are fairly well-to-do and their unmarried teenage daughter becoming pregnant didn't go down well in their social circles. It was better if I just disappeared before anyone found out. I would have been interested to hear their explanation for why I dropped out of school and off the map, but I never got a chance to hear it. I haven't seen them since that day, nor do I want to. I've forgiven them for what they did to me and Zooey, but they're not part of our lives."

"They sent you away?" Seth almost couldn't believe what he was hearing. What kind of parents did that to their child? He had made more than his share of mistakes in his life, but he knew beyond a doubt that his mom and dad would never turn their backs on him, no matter what he did. It was almost inconceivable to even think about. "What did you do?"

"Given that I had no money and nowhere to turn, I am one of the blessed ones. I didn't end up on the street. Instead, I was taken in by a church-run home for teenage mothers. They taught me how to care for my daughter and helped me finish high school and get on my feet. They gave me real-world skills I could use to provide for Zooey and myself. When I was eighteen, I moved to Serendipity, set up shop as an in-home day-care provider, and the rest, as they say, is history."

"Wow. That must have been tough, especially at such a young age. I admire and applaud you for your courage."

Rachel shook her head. "It wasn't courage. I was scared to death. But I had a lot of support. And though Zooey wasn't conceived in an ideal situation, I loved her from the first moment I discovered I was carrying her in my womb. I did what I had to."

"My buddy Luke used to tell me that courage wasn't the lack of fear. It was being afraid and going forward anyway. That's what you did. I call it courage."

Rachel nibbled at her chicken, chewing thoughtfully, her gaze distant. Then, with effort, she seemed to set her emotions aside.

"But enough about me. Tell me about you. Did you join the army right out of high school? Thank you for your service, by the way."

He gave her a clipped nod. He didn't really want to talk about his time in the military, and though appreciative of their acknowledgment, he never knew what to say when people thanked him for serving.

"Like many little boys, I dreamed about becoming a soldier when I grew up," he said. "But I followed through with it and, along with my best friend, Luke Hollister, enlisted before I even finished high school. We were off to boot camp right after we graduated. At the time, I intended to make the army my career. Twenty years and a decent pension sounded good to me. And I really loved serving in the army."

"What happened?" she asked softly.

Seth blew out a breath. "Luke was killed in a firefight. I was right there next to him and—" He swallowed hard to dislodge the memory. "And then a sniper got him. The bullet whizzed right by my ear and hit Luke."

He frowned. It was hard to get the words out.

"That day haunts me. I'll never understand why God let things go down the way they did. I'm a bachelor and yet I was the one who dodged the bullet. Luke left behind his pregnant wife, Tracy, and their ranch land, which has been in the Hollister family for generations."

"It must have been very rough for her," Rachel said. "I remember the prayers that were said for her in church. Such a sad situation. I know what it's like to be pregnant and on your own, but I can't even imagine dealing with the grief she must have felt, on top of having to run the ranch by herself."

Seth nodded his agreement. "Thankfully, Tracy was born and raised on a ranch, so she gradually adapted to becoming the sole owner. I admire her courage so much. She's one of the strongest women I know."

"At least she had her child to look forward to. She had a boy, right?"

"That's right. Little Caden is almost three years old now. I promised Luke I'd watch over Caden and Tracy if anything ever happened to him, which is a big part of the reason I came back to Serendipity before heading off to college. I wanted to check in on them and make sure everything was as okay as Tracy tried to make it sound whenever I spoke to her on the phone. I needed to see her with my own eyes."

"And how is she doing?"

"She appears to be making a success of it, although honestly, I can't even imagine how she does it. She told me straight to my face that she was fine and she didn't need my help, that I should worry about getting my own life in order. I realized then that I didn't want my life to go the same way as Luke's. I didn't re-up in the army, because my heart wasn't in it anymore. I knew I had to do something different."

"I imagine so," Rachel said, sympathy evident in the tone of her voice.

"The truth is, I just want to get away from responsibility for a while. I want to be *me*—to find out who I am outside of the military. I've always had someone else in charge of where I go and what I do in my life. I didn't even take the summer off after high school. Straight from my parents' house into the army, where I was under orders for everything, even eating and sleeping. Right now all I have on my mind is doing my own thing for a change. Make my own decisions without regard to anyone but myself. No strings attached. Saying that aloud makes me sound like a selfish lout, doesn't it?"

"Not at all."

She was generous to say so.

"When I go to college, all I want to worry about is keeping my grades up. That will take some doing. Like I said, I wasn't the best student, but I'm not sure if it's so much that I wasn't good at school as that I didn't really apply myself. I only worked hard enough to keep my grades high enough for sports." He could feel himself flushing with embarrassment. "Aw, man. I sound like a regular slacker. Don't worry—I promise I won't rub off on Zooey."

Rachel laughed. "She could use a little of your good attitude. You certainly sound ready to buckle down and work hard now. So after college, some kind of big-league sports work, and then what?"

"I imagine I'll probably want to settle down at some point—you know, get married and have children. But that is *way* down the road from now, though."

He pressed his lips together. He wasn't even close to being ready for a family of his own. He wasn't financially prepared to support anyone—and frankly, after losing his best friend, he wasn't ready for any relationship that would leave his heart open to getting hurt again.

"But," he continued, forcing the corners of his mouth to curve upward, if only barely, for Rachel's sake, "in other news, I am now the awesome godfather of the cutest baby ever, Luke and Tracy's two-year-old son, Caden. And thanks to my sister and brother-in-law, I'm also the proud uncle of an adorable seven-year-old niece and a feisty pair of twins—one boy and one girl. Samantha and Will's kiddos keep them good and busy."

"So you're the fun uncle, huh?"

He flashed his most charming smile. "Exactly. And that's how I intend to keep things."

"Chief tickler and bogeyman storyteller. The children will look forward to you coming home to visit when you're on breaks at school or the football season is over."

Considering how little they knew of each other, Rachel had just nailed it.

That was the man he wanted to be. The fun uncle who could come and go as he pleased. He was happy to have found someone who seemed to understand where he was at in his life—and why he would soon be leaving town for greener pastures.

Chapter Two

Sunday was usually Rachel's favorite day of the week. It was the only day out of seven that she allowed herself the opportunity to worship, relax and just *be*, after a frantically busy week filled to the brim with toddlers followed by a Saturday crammed with a week's worth of leftover chores and errands.

After Sunday services, she could read or binge on a television series or just nap, which was her favorite way to spend a quiet Sunday afternoon. But today her usual sense of peace had been replaced by a nagging sense of worry.

This morning, she'd watched for Seth at the small church that was home to Serendipity's community of faith. On the day of the auction, they'd agreed to meet after the Sunday service to go over the specific details of when and how he'd work off her auction win, but he hadn't shown up. In fact, none of the Howells had been present, which was unusual, since Seth's parents—Samuel and Amanda—along with Will and Samantha Davenport and their brood usually took up an entire pew.

She'd have to make time to seek Seth out sometime during the week, as soon as possible. Or maybe she could get his cell number from Samantha. She needed the work done without delay. Her day-care recertification was close on the horizon, and from what she'd heard, many of her friends' in-home day cares were failing in favor of corporate-run day cares because of tightening restrictions.

She couldn't afford to fail.

Her business was her lifeline—hers and Zooey's. She couldn't even imagine what she'd do if she lost the ability to take care of the children. It was the only job she'd ever had, the one thing she felt capable of and qualified for.

Rachel didn't regret having Zooey, not for one second, but it *had* put a halt on her college plans and the dreams she'd had for her future. She'd intended to pursue a degree in early childhood education and get her teaching degree.

She'd adapted those dreams into running an in-home day care. Maybe she didn't have the degree behind her name, but she knew she was a good teacher, and the best part of her day was sitting with the kids, reading to them and teaching them letters and numbers.

Every so often she had to pass a government inspection like the one that was coming up in a few weeks. She kept her day care strictly by the code, but the inspectors were becoming more nitpicky.

She had to keep hold of this job, not only because she loved it, but because it paid her bills and she was able to save a little toward her daughter's future.

Zooey came first, and she always would. And that was tied to the other frustration in her life—that her daughter, whom she loved more than anything, was pulling away from her. And the situation kept getting worse.

This morning, Zooey had once again pleaded that she was too sick to go to church, when the truth was she was just trying to get out of going to the Sunday service. It had been happening far too often lately. Usually, Rachel insisted that her daughter accompany her, but she was beyond tired of arguing all the time, so this Sunday she'd given in and allowed Zooey to stay home and sleep in.

As soon as Rachel had walked through the doors of the church, guilt had crushed her. She was the parent in this situation. She needed to be the strong one, no matter how hard Zooey pushed back. She should have required that Zooey come with her—no matter what her flimsy excuses might be.

She wouldn't let it happen again. It didn't matter how tired Rachel was or how much stress she was under, she couldn't shirk her responsibility as a parent. As long as her daughter lived under her roof and ate her food, she was going to go to church on Sundays.

Period.

It wasn't a huge shock to Rachel when she walked in the front door of her modest two-bedroom house and found her daughter playing a video game and talking to someone through her headset. Unfortunately, Rachel had expected it. Zooey didn't even look up—not until Rachel loomed over her with her arms akimbo and a frown on her face.

At least Myst, a black cat with the most extraordinary emerald-green eyes, appeared happy to see her. He threaded in and out of her legs as she stood waiting for Zooey to acknowledge her, his purr sounding like a truck engine.

"I thought you were too sick to go to church," Rachel reprimanded. "And you know you're not allowed to play video games on Sunday."

Even though their family unit was small, Rachel had always tried to make it clear that family time was a priority. In particular, she went out of her way to make Sundays special, a quiet time to spend with her daughter away from the technology that so often drew them apart. She stayed off her phone and computer and she expected Zooey to do the same.

"Sorry, James. I have to go," Zooey said into the headset. "My mom's bugging me."

Rachel stood silently as her daughter turned off her video game, unsure of which part of Zooey's statement she should address first.

The teenager's disrespectful words and behavior or the boy?

"Who is James?" She forced herself to remain calm and not sound accusatory.

"He's just a guy, Mom." She used to know all of Zooey's friends. Though Rachel treasured the time she could spend one-on-one with her little girl, she had always been pleased to welcome any friend who wanted to come over for dinner or join them while they went shopping or to the movies. She'd willingly hosted birthday parties and slumber parties and had enjoyed seeing her happy, social daughter having fun with her friends.

It was only in the past year or so that Zooey had become more secretive over what went on in her life. Her longtime friends rarely came over anymore—she seemed to have taken up with a new crowd that Rachel hadn't met. Meanwhile, her grades had dropped to the point where she had to attend summer school. If Zooey had legitimately had problems with a subject, Rachel would have understood, but Zooey had simply not turned in assignments and, worse, had cut class on more than one occasion.

Though Rachel didn't like to judge, she was responsible for Zooey's safety, and in her opinion, some of her daughter's current friends were questionable at best.

That was what had Rachel worried. She'd raised Zooey to be street-smart as well as book-smart, but she was only sixteen and, whether she wanted to admit it or not, was innocent and vulnerable. Those traits left a girl open to all sorts of predators wanting to take advantage, as Rachel knew all too well.

After all, Rachel's life had drastically changed when *she* was sixteen. She wanted so much more for her own daughter.

"And how do you know this James?" Rachel knew her suspicion was creeping out in her tone. She had heard too many horror stories about creepy men stalking girls online not to worry or to ask questions. She wasn't exactly sure how the game console worked, but she suspected it might be similar to a computer in the ability to connect with strangers. Zooey had been speaking in real time to whoever this James person was. For all Rachel knew, it could be a grown man on the lookout for a girl he could manipulate.

Zooey scowled and defiantly tipped up her chin.

"Check the attitude," Rachel warned.

"He's just a friend. My best friend Lori's boyfriend. Nobody to worry about."

"So you've met him before, then? He's your age? You've seen him face-to-face?"

Zooey sighed overdramatically. "Yes, Mom. He's in summer school with me."

Not so long ago, her daughter had been a sweet little infant curled in her arms. It had been easy to protect and care for her then.

Where had the years gone?

Zooey was old enough to date, although up to this point she'd shown little interest in any particular guy, at least as far as Rachel knew.

Zooey used to talk to her about these things, but lately, not so much. The thought of Zooey dating frightened Rachel more than she could say. She knew it wasn't fair to project her own teenage inadequacies on her daughter, but she couldn't seem to help herself.

Zooey was a different girl from the teenager Rachel had been at her age. Zooey was smart. Confident. Beautiful. Maybe too much so. There was no doubt she would be catching the eyes of Serendipity's young men. And all it would take was one bad decision, one mistake, one misjudgment.

Life could change in an instant. She knew that from her own life and had been reminded of it when she'd been talking with Seth at the auction. Rachel wanted her daughter to be able to be free to chase her dreams, something Rachel had never been able to do, but in order to do that, she had a lot of hurdles to jump.

Rachel had been insecure as a teenager and peer pressure had overwhelmed her. She'd had body-type issues and high school bullies had sometimes fat-shamed her into doing things she would not otherwise have done.

That was how she'd gotten pregnant with Zooey—trying to find someone who would love her for who she was. But the boy had dumped her the moment he found out she was pregnant, accusing her of sleeping around and denying that he was even the father of her child.

He'd never loved her. Looking back, she was pretty sure he'd never even *liked* her. Rachel had found out the truth the hard way.

She didn't want that for her daughter. But she couldn't seem to find a way to express her concerns without sending Zooey on another rant, angry that her mother didn't trust her.

Rachel didn't know how to bridge the gap that was growing between them, but she had to try.

She sat down on the couch, curling one leg underneath her and turning toward her daughter. "I was thinking maybe if you got more involved in church activities, you wouldn't feel so inclined to skip Sunday services."

Zooey twirled a lock of her dark brown hair around her finger and didn't say a word.

"You're really good with my day-care kiddos," Rachel continued. "Maybe you could teach Sunday school when fall comes. The preschoolers would love you. And I'd like to see you go back to youth group this summer. Didn't you used to have a lot of friends there?"

Zooey wouldn't meet her eyes.

She looked—*what*?

Frustrated? Upset? Stricken?

"Zooey?" she prompted when the girl did not speak. "What are you thinking? You can be honest with me."

"I don't want to hurt your feelings," she mumbled.

"This isn't about my feelings. It's about trying to figure out some solutions that will work for both of us."

"Well, I don't want to go to youth group anymore. None of my friends go to church. They think it's stupid."

Rachel felt like someone had slapped her. This was one battle she really didn't want to lose, watching her daughter walk away from the faith she'd been brought up in. But how could she stop Zooey from sliding down that slippery slope?

She pinched the bridge of her nose where another headache was developing.

Peer pressure.

Rachel's breath snagged in her throat. She knew all about peer pressure.

Lord, help me reach my daughter.

"Which friends are those, exactly?" she asked through a tight jaw, barely restraining herself from adding that those friends probably weren't real friends at all if they led her away from church.

"Lori and James. We want to hang out at the community pool and get a good tan once summer school is over. That's where all the cool kids go."

"I see."

She saw all too well. But she didn't know what to do about it.

Push her? Back off?

At least it was just suntanning at the pool.

For now.

"I'm not going to force you to go to youth group, if that's what you're worried about. But you should have been honest with me earlier and told me that you didn't want to go rather than lying about being sick. You don't want to participate? Then don't. But please, be honest with me either way. And don't make your decision based on what your friends think. I've taught you better than that."

Zooey stared at her a moment without speaking. Rachel held her breath, praying she'd gotten through to the rebellious teenager. But when her daughter picked up the headset to the video game console, intending to hook it back up to the system, Rachel felt a sinking certainty that her words hadn't had any impact at all. Reaching out to her daughter wasn't going to work this time. So instead, she'd have to try standing firm. She stopped Zooey with a hand on her arm.

"You may be your own person, but you are sixteen years old and you are living in my house, so I make the rules. No video games on Sunday."

Zooey's face turned red and she dropped the headset onto the coffee table, where it bounced and then clattered onto the wood floor.

"I've had enough of your attitude, young lady."

"Fine." Zooey scowled and then marched straight out the front door.

"Where do you think you are going?" In her frustration, Rachel enunciated every word.

"Out. I'm going out. I can't stand this. I don't want to be around you right now."

"Zooey, stop." It wasn't a suggestion, but the teenager ignored it anyway and shot off down the street on foot, not even bothering to look back.

Rachel huffed out an irritated breath and made to follow her, but just as she was leaving, Seth pulled into her driveway and exited his car—

With a baby in his arms.

* * *

Seth's knees were weak and his gut clenched into knots in an excruciatingly uneven rhythm. His vision felt fuzzy and it was all he could do to plant his feet on the ground, step by agonizing step. The only thing that was keeping him upright was the fact that he was carrying a two-year-old baby in his arms, curled up against his shoulder and sound asleep.

The baby he had vowed to protect, never realizing that one day he would be called to do just that.

Grief sucker punched him, but he willed it back. He had to stay strong for Caden's sake.

"I saw Zooey fly out of here," he said, rocking back and forth on his heels and patting Caden's back. "Is everything all right?"

Rachel nodded, tight-lipped. Her face was flushed red and marked with lines of strain. She didn't look much better than he felt.

"Well…good."

He hesitated. Obviously this wasn't a good time for Rachel. He wasn't even positive why he was here, except for a niggling sensation in the back of his mind that Rachel might be the one person in Serendipity most able to understand what he was going through right now.

She narrowed her gaze on him, studying him intently. "You don't look so good. Would you like to come in?"

"Um, yeah. Thanks."

He followed her through the door and took a seat on the plush armchair. Thankfully, the baby was still sound asleep on his shoulder. Seth hadn't been able to get Caden to stop crying earlier in the day.

He'd tried everything to no avail—changing, feeding,

rocking. Nothing had worked until the little tyke had finally worn himself out.

It was only one of many new challenges he was about to face. Despite the way his family had rallied around him, he'd never felt so alone in his life.

"Would you like some coffee? It'll only take me a minute to make us a pot."

"No, thank you."

She gestured to Caden. "I see you've got Caden with you. I love that he has Luke's blond hair. He's such a sweetheart. Are you babysitting for Tracy today?"

This time he couldn't hold his grief back. It burned like molten lava from his gut to his throat and he had to swallow hard just to speak.

"Tracy's dead."

Rachel's eyes widened and she grasped for the arm of the sofa, shakily seating herself.

"I'm so sorry. I hadn't heard."

"To tell you the truth, I feel numb, like I'm in the twilight zone or something. Yesterday afternoon, she dropped Caden off at my house, saying she had a bad headache. She asked me to watch him. I thought I would only be babysitting for a couple hours."

He blinked hard several times to erase the moisture forming in his eyes.

"Tracy…she…she passed away last night. She didn't just have a headache. She had a brain aneurysm. One second she was here and then she was gone. I've been with my family since yesterday trying to process everything."

"Lord, have mercy." Rachel whispered the prayer. "Poor Tracy. Poor Caden."

Rachel's gaze was full of compassion, but she didn't

speak further, as if she somehow knew he needed to get it all out at once.

"May I?" She stood and held out her arms for Caden, who had awoken and was making tiny sounds of distress.

As soon as Caden was in Rachel's arms, his crying abated. To say the woman was naturally gifted with children would be an understatement. Caden was responding to Rachel way better than he had to Seth or even to Seth's mother or sister throughout the long, grief-filled day.

This was so hard to talk about, or even to think about. The circumstances were surreal.

He felt more helpless at this moment than he had even when he'd seen his best friend gunned down right in front of his eyes.

"You know how the Bible says God won't give you more than you can bear?" he asked, his voice cracking with strain.

She nodded and ran her palm over Caden's silky hair, quietly shushing the baby.

"I don't think that verse is true. I think God has just given me way more than I can handle."

He pulled in a deep breath and continued. "The reading of the will is going to happen directly after the funeral. I already know what's in it. Luke and Tracy appointed me as Caden's guardian should anything ever happen to them, but— I don't know. I never thought it would actually play out this way. After Luke's death... well, I should have realized whole lives can change in a split second. But it's just not something that I wanted to think about, so I put it out of my mind."

"There's no one in Caden's extended family who might be able to take him?"

"No, Luke told me that wasn't an option back when he asked me to be godfather. Luke's parents died in a car crash a few years ago. His grandparents are in an assisted-living facility. Tracy's dad is disabled from a stroke and needs constant care from her mother. They're in no position to raise a child, even their own grandson. Tracy has a sister, Trish, but I've never met her. Luke told me she took off for New York the moment she graduated high school and never looked back. She wasn't at the wedding, and she's never even met Caden, to my knowledge."

He set his jaw to clamp down the emotions roiling through him. "I'm all Caden's got."

"You've got your family to support you."

"Yes, but—" Panic reared and bucked in his chest like a wild stallion. "Luke and Tracy left me the Hollister ranch, as well. It's been in the family for generations. It's Caden's legacy. But I'm not a rancher, Rachel. I hardly even know how to ride a horse, and I don't know the first thing about running a cattle business. I can't *do* this."

Rachel was silent for a moment.

"Of course you can," she said at last.

"No. I...I had plans. I wasn't going to stick around Serendipity. I've already got college lined up, although obviously now there's no way I'm going to go."

His panic was rising steadily in his chest. "I can't be Caden's daddy. I don't know how."

She chuckled mildly. It wasn't a happy sound, but her expression radiated empathy. "Not to quote clichés at you, but you know what they say about the best-laid plans. You'll find a way—a way to take care of Caden and to get your education if you want."

"But a *baby*."

She nodded. "I understand. That's why you've come to me seeking advice. I can empathize with you because I've been there myself. It's mighty intimidating thinking about raising a child on your own. An unplanned pregnancy really threw my life into turmoil, and I was just a kid myself."

Yes.

He'd come here thinking he needed to ask Rachel's help in caring for Caden.

Of course, he needed to get Caden set up in day care so he could spend his days trying to figure out what he was going to do about the ranch. But now he realized it was more than that.

Because she really *did* know what he was going through, the outrageous cyclone of emotions that swirled through him, threatening to blow him away.

He looked her right in the eye. Her gaze was shiny, too, as he expected his own was.

"I am not responsible enough to raise a child," he told her. "I'm only twenty-six myself."

She reached out and touched his arm. The contact somehow grounded him.

Human-to-human.

"I was ten years younger than that when I had Zooey. And I really was all alone. You have your family—and me, if you need me, to help you get your bearings. God brought Caden into your life. He will see you through. It'll take a while, but you'll work this out. For Caden's sake, you have to."

He jerked his chin in a brief nod. He was glad she was straightforward with him instead of couching everything she said in softer language. He desperately needed to be told exactly what to do.

"How?" he asked gravely.

"By taking it one day at a time."

"Sage advice."

But not nearly enough.

"For starters," she continued, "where is Caden sleeping tonight?"

"My place, I guess. I'm staying in one of my mom and dad's cabins. I suppose I'll have to move into the ranch house eventually, but right now, I just can't be there. The memories are too fresh. They hurt too much." He picked off his cowboy hat and threaded his fingers through his hair. "I hadn't really thought about it. I can't seem to think beyond minute to minute, much less one day at a time. How am I going to do this?"

"Stand up," Rachel said, moving to his side. Her voice was strong and determined, as if she were giving him an order. "Now take the baby in your arms."

Seth swallowed hard but did as Rachel bid, tucking a once-again-sleeping Caden against his shoulder. The boy was all toddler, with chubby cheeks and with thick arms and legs, and yet he was so light he seemed to curve right into Seth as he shifted his weight side to side in a rocking motion. The gentle rhythm of the child's breath against his neck soothed Seth as much as the rocking did Caden.

"What are you feeling?" Rachel asked gently.

Seth closed his eyes and breathed in Caden's little-boy scent.

How *did* he feel?

Nervous. Overwhelmed. Panicked. Devastated. And

yet there was something more, something indefinable, hovering just below the surface.

He was responsible for this little human being. And even though it meant his entire life had just been turned upside down and backward, there was something somehow...*right*...about holding Caden in his arms. He couldn't name the emotions, but they were there, cresting in his chest.

"See?" Rachel murmured, even though Seth hadn't answered her question aloud. "Pretty special, isn't it?"

"Mmm," Seth agreed softly, afraid to put his emotions into words.

"I have a mobile playpen that you can use until you have time to outfit yourself better. Caden will be able to eat finger food and finely cut meats, fruits and vegetables. I don't even have to ask if you're a healthy eater, so I imagine you'll have everything you need already stocked in your refrigerator. Do you know how to change a diaper?"

"Caden is in those pull-up ones. My mom showed me how to work them. Although those dirty diapers are going to take some getting used to." He wrinkled his nose at the thought.

"Since you've got the Hollister ranch to worry about, you're probably going to need someone to watch him during the day. Or is your family on that?"

"That's actually why I originally came over. It wasn't to break down on you, I promise."

She laid a reassuring hand on his arm. "I know. It just so happens that I have an opening in my day care, so you can bring Caden over in the morning while you take care of whatever needs doing at the ranch. No charge for the first week while you get on your feet and find the lay of the land. No pun intended."

Her joke drew a slight smile from him. "I can't ask you to do that."

"You didn't ask. I offered. Honestly, things are going to work out. You may not be able to see it now, but God's got it all in His capable hands. Start walking the path, step-by-step, even if you can't see a single thing in front of you. Trust Him to show you the way."

"Mmm," Seth said again. He wasn't sure he believed what Rachel was saying, or even understood all of it, but *she* did, and he didn't want to contradict her when she was doing so much for him.

"You'll have to baby-proof your house right away. Toddlers have the tendency to get into everything and climb on everything. Caden will bump his head and fall to the floor more times than you'll be able to count. But we can at least make the bumps less bumpy and the falls less painful."

We?

Had he really come over only to find day care for Caden, or had God led him over here for more than that? He knew what Rachel would say if he voiced the question aloud. He appreciated her so much for offering her advice and assistance, but again he had trouble forming the words to express his gratitude.

"I know a little bit about baby-proofing. My sister gave me some extra hardware they had left over after putting their own house in order for the twins, but I'm not sure where everything goes or how it works. Samantha or Will can probably help me, but they're busy with the store, so it may be a few days."

"I'm sure they have their hands full with the grocery

and their own kids. I'm free after work tomorrow. I could come over and help you set everything up," she offered.

Caden started hiccuping in his sleep, and Seth and Rachel chuckled softly together.

"I guess this will be an adventure," he admitted. He'd always been one to chase adventure…though he'd never expected to face one quite this huge. There was a big, wide ocean in front of him and he didn't even know how to trim the sails.

But he could learn. And whether it was God or circumstance or whatever, he was grateful for all the support he was receiving. From his family…and from Rachel. What if she hadn't been the one to win him at the auction, telling him her story and putting her in his head as someone he could turn to in this situation? He didn't even want to think about that.

"Adventure is a good way to look at it," she said. "You and Caden are a team."

He looked down at the still-hiccuping but soundly sleeping little boy in his arms and his heart welled.

He wouldn't let Caden down, no matter what.

He was Caden's permanent legal guardian and would be the only parent the boy would ever know.

It was what Luke and Tracy would have wanted. It was what Caden needed. And it was what Seth was determined to be.

A father.

Chapter Three

One day at a time.

Rachel was great at doling out counsel but not so much at putting it to use in her own life.

Seth was trying to figure out how to parent Caden—and he was looking to *her* for advice?

She felt as if someone had stamped a giant fail sign on her forehead. What use was she going to be to Seth—or Caden—when she didn't have her own house in order?

Actually, helping Seth was a good way to get out of her own head for a while, to forget the constant bickering that had taken over her relationship with Zooey. At least she knew what to do with Caden.

She had to admit she was looking forward to Seth bringing sweet Caden over for day care. Rachel loved children of all ages, but there was something about a pudgy toddler, just learning to strike out on his own and explore the world, that really captured Rachel's heart.

And Caden would need all the extra love and attention she could give him. He was fortunate to have such a dedicated guardian in Seth, and he had Seth's extended family to offer strength and support. He was going to be okay, but Rachel still grieved over the circumstances that had left this boy without his mother and father.

And yet she saw something in Seth—his dedication and determination—that made her think he would turn out to be a fine father for Caden in the long run.

Seth had entrusted her with Caden's day care, and she was resolved to do everything she could to make Seth's transition from *footloose and fancy-free* to *father and rancher* as streamlined and painless as possible.

In some ways it would be easier for Caden than for Seth. Caden would adapt quickly. Poor Seth knew next to nothing about child care and had admitted he understood little about ranching, either.

And now, in the space of one day, he had a child and owned a ranch.

Talk about a learning curve.

Rachel poured herself a cup of coffee and went out to sit on the front porch and enjoy the early morning. Seth would be coming a bit earlier than the other parents so he and Caden would have more time to adjust to their first day.

Most of the time it was harder on the parents than it was on the children to let go that first day. Given Seth's peculiar situation, she suspected it might be even more difficult for him. His life had undergone so many changes so quickly he probably didn't know which way was up anymore.

Putting everything else aside, she felt sure he was mourning the loss of a sweet, lovely woman who had died far too soon. It was clear Seth had considered Tracy a friend, and her death would have been a shock to him even if Caden hadn't been in the picture, especially on top of the grief he still experienced over Luke's death. Caden was all Seth had left of his friends to hold on to. Rachel wondered if it would be difficult for him to let the boy go, even for just a few hours.

As for Caden, he might be too young to understand the whole truth of what had happened, but in his own way, he had to be wondering where his mama had gone and why she wasn't coming back to get him. Rachel was certain he must be missing her terribly.

She fought back the tears that sprang to her eyes. She needed to be strong for both Caden and Seth.

Her cat, Myst, diverted her attention when he appeared and flopped by her side, his purr like the deep revving of an engine as he groomed himself. Myst would make himself scarce for the rest of the day, having learned the hard way to avoid overexcited toddlers with grabby hands. He was a typical feline, antisocial to most humans except when he wanted to be snuggled and petted on his own terms, and even then he graced only Rachel and Zooey with that honor.

Mr. Picky was his nickname.

Rachel had just finished her coffee when Seth pulled his car into her driveway. She stepped forward to help him release Caden from his car seat. She laughed, her heart welling, when the little boy wrapped his arms around her neck and squeezed tightly.

"This ridiculous thing is more complicated than it looks," Seth said of the five-point buckle. "It took me forever to figure it out the first time."

"Car seats are one of my many areas of expertise," she teased, but Seth nodded solemnly.

"I imagine so."

A lump burned hot in her throat. It didn't take a

genius to realize he was thinking about all the things he *didn't* know about raising a child, and Rachel mentally kicked herself for her insensitivity.

She was relieved when he changed the subject.

"If you have a moment, would it be okay for me to take a look at your backyard and the play equipment you currently have?" he asked, leaning down to scoop Myst into his arms. He stroked the cat, who in turn nuzzled under his chin, demanding his complete devotion and attention. "We can discuss your needs and then I will draw up some preliminary suggestions on how best to make this work."

"How did you do that?" she asked, so stunned she forgot to answer his question.

"Do what?"

"Myst doesn't like anybody, especially men."

He scratched the cat's ears and chuckled. "Cats like me. I don't know why. I've never had one of my own. Hopefully, I have the same effect on horses and cows."

Seth was such a charmer that Rachel suspected he might have that effect on every living creature he came in contact with, including every pretty young lady who crossed his path, and most of the older ones, too. Cats were especially intuitive, and Myst obviously thought highly of Seth.

But as far as the play yard went—

"Don't worry about building anything for me. I'm officially absolving you of any obligation. You have way too much going for you to be concerned about my needs."

She was worried about what she'd be able to do, with the recertification coming up so rapidly, but it wasn't fair to bring Seth in on it. He'd just landed himself a baby. That took precedence over any problems she was experiencing.

She'd just have to figure out how to handle this herself. The most logical thing to do would be to break down the old play equipment on her own and rent a trash bin one weekend to get rid of all the pieces. She could clean up the backyard well enough to pass the inspection. New equipment would have to wait.

"No, Rachel. Let me do this for you. You're helping me out so much by caring for Caden and with all the instructions you've given me."

He made it sound as if she were a how-to manual. The thought made her smile.

"You'll be paying me for the day care, remember? Although like I said earlier, don't forget that the first week is on the house."

"And you paid for *me* at the auction," he shot back. He gestured toward the door. "I mean it. I don't mind building you a new play yard. I know you said you have someone coming to assess the day care soon for recertification. This is important to you—and honestly, I think it will be good for me. Building a project like a playhouse that I know I'll excel in will take my mind off all the stuff I *don't* know how to do. So you see, you're doing me a favor."

She didn't see how he could possibly smile after all he'd been through in the past twenty-four hours, but the toothy grin he flashed her worked its charm.

She was not immune.

How could she say no?

With Caden still in her arms, she led Seth out to the backyard and then let the toddler down to play while she talked to his new guardian.

She gestured to her current play equipment, a combination of wood, pipes and canvas that included a tent, a slide and a couple of swings.

"I've been told I have to remove or replace it by the beginning of July. At this point I'm thinking that removing it is going to be challenge enough in itself."

"I can probably hack it down in half a day," Seth said, setting Myst on the ground at his feet. The cat wound in a figure eight around his legs, his tail curling around his black cowboy boots in a ploy for more attention. "And then, once we've settled on something you like, it's just a matter of ordering in the materials. I can probably build something new in a weekend—if you're willing to watch Caden for me, that is."

"That's a given," she assured him, pointing to where Caden was scaling a kid-sized slanted climbing wall. "Look at that little boy crawl. If I didn't know better— It's almost as if he's related to you."

Seth's brow lowered and his lips tightened, but his smile remained. "Yeah. Well, I guess Caden is related, kind of, or at least he will be when I formally adopt him."

"That's for sure the direction you're going, then?"

He nodded. "It's what Luke and Tracy would have wanted. And it's what I want to do."

"You're a good friend. And you'll be a great father."

"Your lips to God's ears," he murmured.

Seth had formed a plan, kind of. He could see no way around it but that he accept that he was Caden's permanent legal guardian. He needed to adopt Caden as his own and be his *father*—and then somehow he had to keep the Hollister ranch up and running for Caden's legacy.

He'd considered every other possibility and had come up with nothing. As he'd told Rachel, adopting Caden was what Luke and Tracy would have wanted.

How could he do less?

So much for the carefree days of being his own man. He knew it was not only immature but irresponsible even harboring that moment of regret, but there it was. He let it flow through him...and then he let it go.

Making decisions with only his own happiness in mind was a thing of the past. Period. Now his life belonged to Caden, and under the circumstances, that was exactly as it should be.

He would do everything in his power to be the father Caden needed him to be, despite that the thought sent shivers down his spine and he was looking at a learning curve that was a series of hairpin turns down a steep mountain road.

The more time he spent with Caden, the more he admired Rachel for the success she'd made out of her life. A bright, intelligent daughter. A thriving business that she loved.

Before having a toddler of his own to take care of, he never would have comprehended all of the sacrifices Rachel, as a single mother, had made—and continued to make—for Zooey's sake.

Big things like not going to college. Little everyday things like cooking meals and playing blocks with her on the carpet.

Now that he was in a similar situation, he'd become minutely aware of just how much parents, especially single parents, acted and sacrificed for their children's sake on a constant, daily basis. It didn't matter if the child was two or twenty. A parent would always be a parent.

He would always be Caden's dad. It still sounded odd to think of himself that way, but there it was.

Friday of the first week had finally come, and Caden's introduction to day care had gone well. Rachel had reported that he had no trouble fitting in with the other children. He was a social child and especially enjoyed snack time. And to Seth's amazement, Caden always appeared as happy to see him at the end of the day as Seth was to see Caden. The baby still had moments when he'd cry uncontrollably. Seth thought he must be missing his mama. But they were coping, he and Caden, moving forward together, step by step.

Seth was anxious for this particular workday on the ranch to end. He'd thought he was in good physical shape before all these new challenges in his life began, but at the moment he was sore head to toe from all his hours on horseback, and his brain was aching from the amount of new information he was trying to consume all at once.

Who knew that running a ranch would be so complicated?

Though he'd grown up in a ranching community, he hadn't ever been so much as a weekend cowboy, and aside from half listening to the complaints of friends in school, he'd never thought about cows.

All he knew was that ranchers roamed the range herding cattle to new pastures as the old grass got eaten up.

His learning curve with the ranch was nearly as complex as the one with Caden. Thankfully, Tracy's foreman, Wes Gorman, was a kind, knowledgeable older man who'd spent his entire life as a working cowboy and who was willing to keep things running while he taught Seth the ropes of the business.

Seth would have laughed at his unintended pun except his backside was so saddle sore he wasn't sure he could conjure a smile. He'd be sitting on ice for a week.

He felt like a fraud in his hat and boots, although he'd worn both from the time he hit high school. Nearly all the men in Serendipity wore cowboy hats. But then again, nearly all of them were ranchers.

He'd sometimes ridden the range with Luke when they were boys, but they'd never done much real ranch work. They'd always been too busy goofing around. He vaguely remembered the freedom he'd felt when he'd galloped across the meadow back when he was a teenager, but he hadn't been anywhere near a horse in a decade.

He was more cautious now than he was when he was a hormone-ridden high schooler. He wasn't about to gallop anywhere and risk breaking his neck, thank you.

Still, he was determined to learn everything there was to know about the Hollister family's ranch, Bar H, and that started with hands-on experience at everything from riding out and evaluating the herd to mucking out the horse stalls.

He was proud of his progress so far. He hadn't lost his seat in the saddle—*yet*—although he was careful to keep his mount, Luke's old chestnut gelding, Windsong, from moving any faster than a trot. He had spent the first couple of days surveying the Bar H holdings and becoming acquainted with both horses and cattle. Wes had explained to him about rotating the grazing stock among the fields and pastures and that the cattle were beef cows.

He had yet to learn how to balance the books, which was on the docket for the weekend, but at least that could be done from a desk. He would be glad to be seated on something that didn't move, for a change.

He wasn't looking forward to wrestling with numbers. Math had been a weak spot in school. But if he was going to run the Bar H property right, he was going to have to understand the financial status of the ranch.

When he pulled Windsong up to the old barn, exhausted and ready to slip out of the saddle and take a long, hot shower to soothe his weary muscles, he was surprised to find Rachel already there waiting for him.

She had agreed to bring Caden to him today rather than him picking the boy up, but he hadn't intended for her to meet him at the stable. No sense everyone getting dusty and mud caked. They had planned to meet later at Seth's house so she could help him finish baby-proofing, and he was stoked to show her the designs he'd drawn up for her new play equipment.

She didn't immediately see him approach and he reined to a halt, watching the interplay between woman and toddler with interest. She was holding Caden by the hands as he hopped on and off a square bale of hay. Rachel displayed unending patience as Caden wanted to jump again and again. They were both giggling as she picked him up, twirled him around in circles and tickled his tummy.

The stress lines usually so prominent around her eyes and mouth eased as she played with Caden. Seth had always thought Rachel was pretty, but she simply lit up like an evergreen at Christmas when she was around children, especially Caden.

She had a special gift, and he was beyond grateful she had won him at the auction. *Someone* was watching out for him, and in the deep confines of his heart he knew it was the Lord.

How else could he explain having been so fortunate? Rachel was giving Seth back at least as much as he would be able to do for her in building her new playhouse, and she'd spent money for his efforts.

What she did for him, and for Caden, she did out of the kindness of her heart and nothing more.

Rachel caught sight of him and stopped twirling around, settling Caden on her hip and pointing to Seth, who was still on board Windsong.

"Look who just rode in, Caden."

Seth grinned and tipped his hat to her.

"It's your cowboy father. Er...is that what you're going to have him call you? Father?"

His gaze widened, the burden of responsibility weighing even more heavily on his shoulders as he realized that was just one more decision he had to make, out of the hundreds he'd already made and the millions more ahead of him.

"I haven't even had a chance to really think about it. I've been talking to my lawyer about the steps I'll need to take to legally adopt him as my son, so I guess that would be an important step."

"And probably the sooner, the better, so Caden can get used to it. What do you think? *Father? Dad? Daddy? Pop?*"

"I called my own father *Daddy*, at least when I was a little tyke like Caden. I'd feel honored to follow in my father's footsteps—and hope to be able to do half as good a job as he did parenting Samantha and me. We were a handful."

"Did you hear that, Caden?" Rachel raised the toddler from her hip to seat him in the saddle in front of Seth. "Do you want your *daddy* to take you on a horsey ride?"

Caden squealed with delight and pumped his arms and legs with such joyful abandon that Seth could barely contain him in the saddle, never mind keep Windsong steady. Fortunately, the horse was calm and patient. Seth wasn't a great horseman yet, but somehow he managed to walk the horse around the corral a couple of times.

He couldn't contain the smile that split his face. He knew Caden's excitement was over being on a large animal well off the ground, but his own heart was internally performing the same squealing pump-and-wiggle dance.

Daddy.

So *this* was what it was like to care for another person more than he cared for himself. A peculiar array of emotions slammed into him so suddenly and so intensely that it was all he could do to keep his back straight and his boots in the stirrups as he continued to lead Windsong around the corral with Caden propped securely just behind the saddle horn.

Despite the tragedy that had put them here, he and Caden were now a family. He would love and cherish this little piece of humanity with everything in him.

All of a sudden, Caden wasn't a burden.

He was a blessing.

"Say *horsey*," Rachel said, waving to get Caden's

attention as she snapped a picture with her cell phone. She held it up so Seth could see what she'd taken.

"There you go, you two. Your first family photo."

Chapter Four

"Has Seth asked you out on a date yet?" Zooey teased as she helped Rachel unhook the swings from the old swing set in anticipation of tearing the entire thing down.

It had been a crazy week with Seth learning to be a new father. Rachel had spent several evenings with him, sometimes working on modifying his apartment, other times simply enjoying playing with the toddler.

She'd told him multiple times that he didn't need to worry about her backyard plans, that she'd find another way to get the work done on her play set, but he'd insisted on starting on his project on this bright Saturday morning in June.

To Rachel's relief, Zooey was in a good mood for a change and had even offered to help break down all of the day care's old playground equipment. Rachel suspected that Zooey's good mood had more to do with the fact that Seth and Caden were on their way than any genuine desire to help her mother.

But at this point Rachel was grasping at straws with the girl and would take whatever pleasant interaction she could get, even with strings attached. Zooey had really taken to Caden in the past week, giving the toddler extra attention when she wasn't attending summer school. If Rachel had to use Seth and Caden as bait in order to spend more time with her daughter without it turning into an argument, so be it.

"No," Rachel answered, using a hand drill to remove some of the screws that held the play set together. She was both systematic and judicious, not wanting the whole set to collapse on top of her before Seth arrived to direct the project. "Seth has *not* asked me out. And he's not going to. I would appreciate it if you wouldn't mention the harebrained scheme you and Lizzie came up with at the auction. I already came clean with him and told him all about it, so there's no sense bringing it up again and putting him—well, everyone, really—in an awkward position, right?"

Zooey shrugged. "I don't see how you two going out on a date would be awkward. It might just be nice, you know. Dinner and a movie? How long has it been, Mom, since you've been in a relationship? I mean, really."

Too long.

Rachel wouldn't even know what to do on a date or how to act. She felt certain it would be *beyond* awkward.

Especially if her date was Seth.

"Give the poor man a break. He just found out he's going to be an adoptive father. He doesn't have time to be asking women out on dates."

"But that's what makes you two a perfect match. Single mom. Single dad. Totally gorgeous guy. Pretty woman. Mom, really. What more could you ask for?"

"For you to keep your nose out of my business,"

Rachel replied promptly, wrinkling her nose at her daughter.

Zooey sputtered out a laugh, knowing Rachel was teasing. She didn't sound at all convinced.

"I'm not looking for a relationship right now, and he's definitely not. He's barely keeping his head above water with all that has just gotten dumped on him."

"Then he needs a woman's help now more than ever. You'd be great for him, Mom. I know you would." She paused and frowned, her forehead wrinkling as if she were pondering some great thought. "You should be in the market for a husband, or at least a boyfriend. Why aren't you?"

"In a relationship? When would I have time to date? Between operating my day care and raising you—"

"Mom," Zooey protested, the word sharp and piercing. "I'm sixteen."

Precisely the point, Rachel thought but didn't dare say aloud.

Boys. Dating. Parties. Peer pressure. She needed to keep a closer eye on her daughter than ever.

"I know you don't want to think about it, but I'm not going to be around forever," Zooey continued. "College is only a couple of years away and then I'll be off living my own life. What are you going to do then?"

Zooey's words jabbed Rachel's heart. She knew them to be true and right—the way life should be—but that didn't make it any easier. She'd spent half her life caring for her daughter. What would it be like when she was gone?

Lonely.

For the single mother, it was the empty-nest syndrome in spades.

She didn't know what to say to Zooey. She didn't want her daughter to worry about her when she should be thinking about her future.

Relief rushed through her when Seth let himself into the backyard through the side gate she'd unlocked for him.

"Good morning, pretty ladies," he called.

Whew. Saved by the bell—or rather, the handsome man. Now she wouldn't have to continue with the excruciating task of answering Zooey's question—especially because she had no idea *what* her future would look like when Zooey struck out on a life of her own. She'd been so focused on securing Zooey's future that she had neglected her own.

It was a sobering thought, but one she couldn't dwell on. Not with Seth here.

Seth would have caught any woman's eye this morning, not just Rachel's. He had changed up his look, favoring a black T-shirt that hugged his muscular frame and a Texas Rangers baseball cap, along with bright blue running shoes rather than his usual cowboy hat and boots.

He was holding a squirming Caden under his arm like a football, just above the tool belt strapped around his waist. Rachel's first and natural instinct was to dash forward and correct Seth for the way he held the boy, but then she realized both he and the toddler were making zooming noises while Caden stretched his arms out like the wings of an airplane.

It was a very guy kind of thing to do, and it warmed her heart to see the way the handsome suddenly-a-cowboy-daddy and Caden were bonding.

"Not a word to Seth about what we've been talking

about," Rachel cautioned Zooey from under her breath as Seth put the little boy on the ground. Rachel cast a sidelong look at her daughter to make sure she'd been listening.

If she saw so much as a mischievous sparkle in Zooey's eyes, she was immediately going to send her on an errand to pick up...*something*...she needed right away.

From Australia.

As it turned out, Rachel needn't have worried. The moment Zooey spotted Caden, she rushed forward and swept the toddler into her arms, asking him if he wanted to dig in the sand with her.

The oversize sandbox contained not only shovels and pails but a large collection of toy dump trucks, bulldozers and a toddler-sized backhoe to scoop the sand up and into the backs of the trucks.

Zooey wasn't the type of teen to worry too much about fashion or invest in clothes that had to be kept immaculate. Dressed in jeans and a baggy bright green T-shirt, she sank on her knees into the sand and pulled Caden onto her lap, showing him how to use a bulldozer to push the sand into a pile and then scoop it up with the backhoe and haul it around with a dump truck. To Caden's delight, she even made truck noises to go along with the various movements.

Rachel shook her head at the incredible sight.

If she didn't know better, she would never have guessed that Zooey was an only child with no brothers and sisters to play in the sandbox with. She'd always interacted regularly with Rachel's day-care children, but the scene playing out before her somehow went beyond anything in Zooey's past.

She and Caden almost appeared to be brother and

sister, even with the age gap between them. Zooey was clearly taken with Caden, and the little boy was smitten with her, as well. It was the cutest thing to watch, and Rachel's heart warmed.

After a brief discussion with Seth, she waved at Zooey. "Seth and I are going to unload some more tools from the back of his truck. Are you going to be okay with Caden for a few more minutes?"

Zooey grinned, her face beaming with delight. "We're fine right here, aren't we, Caden?"

Caden giggled and tossed a handful of sand into a nearby bucket.

Rachel's throat pinched and she snagged in a breath. It was a poignant moment, watching Zooey and the toddler having fun together.

"Wow," Seth said with a low whistle as he and Rachel headed out front. "Like mother, like daughter, huh? She definitely picked up your nurturing genes. Look how great she's doing with Caden. She's a real natural at this. You can tell Caden already loves her."

"I agree," Rachel said. "She's always had a special gift for children."

Her memories were bittersweet.

"From the time she was about four years old, she started helping me out in my day care. At first she'd just play with the kids, but as she got older, she'd read to them, feed them snacks, give them hugs if they fell down and scraped their knees. She'd bandage them up and kiss all their owies away."

"Sounds like maybe she'd make a good doctor," he commented as he sorted through some of his tools.

Rachel sighed. "I used to think so, too, until she hit Algebra II and didn't pass the course. I'm not sure if it's because math is not her thing, or if she just wasn't applying herself. I believe that part of it is that she lost interest in doing well in school."

And she started hanging out with a questionable group of friends who influenced her in a bad way, but Rachel wasn't about to admit that aloud.

"I guess who can really blame her, right?" Seth said, chuckling. "Algebra II is when they start you on imaginary and irrational numbers, isn't it? Why in the world would you want to work with irrational numbers? And don't even get me started on imaginary. If they aren't real, why would you want to do equations with them?"

"I excelled in language arts and literature when I was in school," she agreed. "*Irrational* and *imaginary* apparently have entirely different definitions to science nerds."

Seth belted out a laugh. "Good point."

He grabbed a couple of sawhorses and leaned them against the truck, then handed her a circular saw.

"Careful. It's a little heavy," he warned her as he picked up the sawhorses and carried them, one under each arm.

The saw *was* heavy and was awkward in her grasp, much like how her emotions played out nearly every time Seth was in her presence.

Heavy and awkward.

She liked him, and she liked being around him. Most of the time she felt comfortable with him, but she couldn't always account for her feelings when their eyes met and her stomach flipped or a spark of electricity zapped through her.

That, she was keeping a major secret. If Zooey ever even suspected Seth had a crazy effect on her, she would never hear the end of it. Besides, it wasn't like it was a big deal. He was an attractive man. There was nothing strange or unusual in noticing that, particularly when she had no intention of doing anything about it.

"I don't know that I had a favorite subject in high school, but I did enjoy playing sports."

"Which one?"

He chuckled. "Oh, all of them. I especially liked track and soccer. I hadn't grown into my full height yet, so football was something of a challenge for me. My smaller frame had its advantages, though. I was a decent running back, and I could slip through the lines because of my size. I would pretty much do anything as long as I was outside running in the fresh air and not cooped up in a stale classroom."

She could easily imagine Seth as a youth, antsy and squirrelly and not wanting to feel boxed in by four walls. Maybe that was why parkour appealed to him so much. He could jump on the walls rather than be smothered by them.

"I don't know why the school system thinks it needs to torture every one of its students with upper-level math. Who actually uses that stuff?"

"Right?" he agreed, shaking his head. "I mean, I suppose if you want to be a chemist or a rocket scientist, you need to know equations and formulas and Xs and Os."

She laughed at his misuse of algebraic formulas. She'd never seen an equation with XO before.

"I don't believe I've ever seen an O in a mathematical formula, though I have seen some at the bottom of a love letter." She blushed. "On television, I mean."

She sped forward so as to cover her own embarrassment. She'd never received a love letter in her life.

"Honestly, I've never used algebra at all," she said, "other than solving for a single X, which comes in handy when I'm missing one variable of a real-life equation. Otherwise, I don't use upper math. Ever."

"Me neither. I've got to say, I am freaking out about keeping the books at the Bar H ranch. I'm not sure I can afford to hire a regular accountant, but I don't know how I am going to be able to get along without one."

"Let me help you," Rachel offered. "I've always done my own books for the day care. I can show you how to use the spreadsheets you'll need for taxes and work with you until you're comfortable doing it on your own."

"I can't ask you to do that."

"You didn't. I offered. And it's no big deal, especially after all you're doing for me with the playhouse. Just let me know when it's convenient for you and we'll take a look at your ledgers together. I'm not familiar with the business side of ranching, but tallying income and expenses is the same no matter what kind of business you're running."

"It's not paper ledgers. It's some computer program that's supposed to make things easier. So far I haven't found that to be the case. It may as well all be written in Greek for all the good it does me."

"Trust me. Once you learn the program, entering or scanning your numbers into the computer is *way* easier than using a paper ledger, like I had to do when I first started my day care. The computer does all the hard calculations for you."

"If you say so."

She didn't know how the conversation had gone from Zooey and Caden to accounting, but after seeing Seth's relieved expression when she said she would assist him, she was glad they'd set off on that particular bunny trail.

She wanted to help him, however she could, and it wasn't just because he was helping her prepare her day care to pass inspection.

His success was Caden's success, and that little boy deserved the best.

"If you ever find a use for upper arithmetic, be sure to let me know," she teased. "I've been around longer than you and I've never seen it."

"You make it sound like you're ancient. You're not exactly an old lady. What are you, maybe—"

"Stop right there, mister." She nearly dropped the circular saw in order to hold up a hand. "Haven't you ever been told not to guess at a woman's age?"

He shrugged. "I'm just telling it how I see it."

"Let's just say I'm older than you. And I've seen a lot in my...*years*."

Rachel didn't miss the flash of sorrow and grief that crossed Seth's gaze and immediately began to apologize.

"I'm so sorry. That was a thoughtless remark for me to make. You may be a few years younger than me, but I know you've seen and experienced the world in ways I never have. It's not like you're fresh out of high school. I imagine two tours in the military made you grow up pretty fast."

She didn't mention Luke's and Tracy's deaths, but she knew they were heavy on Seth's heart.

With effort, he turned his frown into a smile. "Yeah. Well, that may be true. I have seen a lot, and not all of it good. But I don't like to think about those times, much less talk about them. Anyway, my biggest challenge ever is right in front of me, hanging out in the sandbox getting ready to—"

With a choked squeak, he dropped the sawhorses with a clatter and dashed toward Caden, who was pumping his arms, clumps of sand in both tiny fists.

Seth snatched Caden from the sandbox and brushed the sand from his fists.

"No, Caden. We don't eat sand." His voice sounded hoarse and frantic.

Zooey giggled. "I don't think he was going to eat it. Throw it at me, maybe. I've been trying to teach him not to do that. But don't worry. I've been keeping a close eye on him. He hasn't put any sand in his mouth."

Blowing out a breath in relief, Seth shifted Caden to one arm and picked off his ball cap, then scrubbed his fingers through his dark hair, leaving the tips in jagged peaks. He groaned in exasperation, seemingly more at himself than at Caden or Zooey.

"No, I know. You have a lot more experience with toddlers than I do, Zooey. Sorry. I shouldn't have freaked out on you. It was a gut reaction. And not a very good one."

"He'll get more sand in his shoes than in his mouth, I assure you," Rachel teased, amused by the look of sheer horror that crossed Seth's face.

"I'm kidding." She set the circular saw down in a safe corner next to the playhouse and away from the sandbox and laid a reassuring hand on his arm. "Well, I'm half kidding, anyway. I highly suggest you make a habit of removing his shoes or boots over a trash can whenever you leave a sandpit."

She chuckled. "I learned the hard way the first time I

took Zooey's shoes off after a jaunt on the playground. She was lying across my bed. I had to wash the comforter twice to get all the sand out of it."

"Right. Empty his shoes over the trash can. Don't get sand on the bed. Got it." He sounded as if he was adding her latest words of guidance to an already-enormous mental list. "Any other sage advice you want to give me?"

"Only one thing."

"And what is that?" His brow furrowed in concentration. She knew a grown man wouldn't want to be thought of as adorable, but that was exactly the adjective that flashed across Rachel's mind at his determined expression.

"Relax. Take a breath. You're going to be okay. Caden is going to be okay. Of course, there will be bumps and bruises along the road. Trips and falls. No one is a perfect parent, Seth, so don't beat yourself up when things don't go quite as you anticipated. You'll make mistakes. Caden will take a spill and scrape his knees, and you'll be there to pick him up, clean him off, put a bandage on his owie and kiss it better. And then life will go on."

"But what if—" He put his ball cap back on his head, with the brim facing backward this time. He released a breath and groaned. "This is hard."

Rachel nodded. She wanted to chuckle but resisted, knowing how serious Seth was at this moment.

"Yes, it is. Parenting is the toughest job ever, but it is one of the most rewarding things you'll ever do. Zooey is the light of my life."

She spoke loud enough for Zooey to hear the compliment, but her daughter suddenly appeared more interested in bulldozing sand toward Caden's dump truck. Rachel hoped Zooey knew she meant what she said.

Rachel envied Seth the toddler years. Toddlers, she could handle. Zooey had never gone through the terrible-twos stage. Rachel might have had to struggle to make ends meet, but she'd never had any issues with Zooey acting up. As she'd told Seth, Zooey was her biggest blessing. Motherhood was hard, but even as a baby, Zooey had been an endless source of joy that made all the work so very worth it.

Teenage years, on the other hand—she was *so* out of her depth there.

But it was Seth's relationship with Caden they were discussing.

"One more thing."

"Yeah? What's that?" He was busy brushing granules of sand from the spaces between Caden's fingers and didn't glance up at her.

"Don't worry if a little sand makes it into Caden's mouth from time to time. He'll learn fairly quickly that it doesn't taste good. Right now he's just exploring his world with all of his senses."

Which was much less complicated than watching a vulnerable teenager who thought she already knew everything explore hers. If only sand in the mouth was Rachel's largest concern.

"Right," Seth agreed, plunking Caden back down in the sandbox. "Don't worry so much. Got it."

He trusted her judgment. That meant a lot.

He bent down to retrieve the sawhorses he'd dropped earlier and set them up, then surveyed the old play set with a practiced eye.

"Why don't you start removing all the plastic pieces—the slides and climbing ladders," he suggested. "I'll work on the wood. We may be able to salvage some of this stuff to share with others for their woodstoves. It's not cold now, of course, but once the chill of winter sets in, folks will be glad to have a little extra wood on their piles. I don't know exactly what would be the best way to distribute it, but I'm sure we can come up with something."

She flashed him a warm smile. There was nothing more attractive in a man than a heart for serving others—friends and neighbors, and especially the baby that had been given into his care.

Warning sirens were blaring; lights were flashing in vivid colors.

Warning. Warning. Attraction alert.

She scrambled back to the subject at hand.

"What a great idea. I suggest we stack the scrap pieces just outside of the church for people to take as they have need for them."

His gaze widened. "I hadn't thought of the church. It makes sense, though, since nearly everyone in town attends Sunday services. And we can have Jo put the word out about where to find the wood for those that don't regularly visit the chapel."

Good idea, particularly because she knew that Seth had been one of those Christmas and Easter Christians who rarely darkened the door of the little community church for the past several years. Now, after losing his friends, faith might be even more of a struggle for him. She prayed God would work on Seth's heart through everything he'd experienced and not have him turn away based on what he'd seen and gone through.

She couldn't even begin to imagine having to deal with everything that had happened to him. All she knew was that God's light had found her during her darkest moments, and He could do the same for Seth.

In the meantime, she would strive to be a living witness of God's love for him.

"You know, Rachel," Seth said, breaking into her thoughts, "there's one thing you said to me this morning that's still eating at me."

"What's that?"

She tensed. His tone made it sound as if she'd said something wrong. She hoped she hadn't said anything that would lead him off the path of grace.

"You said you felt like an old lady." He frowned and shook his head. "As if."

"Believe me, I do."

Ancient.

Prehistoric, even.

Seth gave her a slow and thorough once-over, head to toe and then back again—a very *masculine* and appreciative examination. His midnight-blue eyes blazed into hers and a half smile curved slowly up one side of his lips.

A shiver ran down her spine, and while it felt unfamiliar to her, it was not altogether unpleasant. Those warning sirens in her head weren't sounding loud enough to stop these feelings or even slow them down.

She was in trouble.

"Trust me," he said, his voice dipping to a lower octave. "You are *so* not over the hill. Not that you really could be at—what?—twenty-nine?"

"I thought we'd already covered this ground. It is rude to ask a woman's age or even to guess at it."

He barked out a laugh. "I'm not asking. Just sayin'.

From my viewpoint, you've got a good long way before you reach old anything."

She didn't know how to respond to the glittering look in Seth's eyes, never mind the admiration he'd verbally heaped on her.

This—the slightest hint of *this*—wasn't supposed to be happening. She shouldn't be thinking about Seth as a…well, as a *man*…much less reacting to him as a woman. Years earlier, after a few disastrous attempts to try dating as a single mom, she'd made the decision to focus on her daughter, her work and her church. Those were her priorities, and dating had no place in them. Zooey and Lizzie had put silly ideas into her head and now she was imagining all kinds of things that didn't exist, thoughts that shouldn't be so much as flashing through her mind, never mind lodging there.

Get ahold of yourself, Rachel, she mentally coached herself. *Get off this slippery slope before someone gets hurt. Before* you *get hurt.*

She could make a mile-long list of the reasons she shouldn't be attracted to Seth and why she was all wrong for him even if there was a certain physical and emotional chemistry between them.

They were opposites in every conceivable way. He swung from the trees and somersaulted over benches. She was lucky if she could make it through a round of push-ups and sit-ups while she worked out with her in-home DVDs. A couple of flights of stairs winded her. Seth could probably climb Mount Everest.

His life was all about health and fitness, whereas hers…*wasn't.*

He'd seen the horrors of war in the worst way, with his best friend being shot down right in front of him, and yet he made it a habit to build his world on the positive, the cup half-full. She had to be careful not to get down on herself and view the world under a gray and miserable thundercloud.

Seth sometimes acted immature for his age. Rachel acted too old for hers. The six-year gap between them might as well be a chasm without a bridge, one that was impossible to cross.

Most important, Seth had recently inherited both a baby and a ranch. It was all he could do just to adapt to his new roles, though he was nothing if not determined.

She couldn't help thinking of the way he panicked when he thought Caden might be in danger of eating sand and somehow hurting himself with it. How he proudly rode his soon-to-be-officially-adopted son around on his horse. The picture of him cradling Caden in his strong arms with such tenderness that even now, at the mere thought of it, tears pricked in Rachel's eyes.

Seth's plate was full to overflowing, and that was the biggest hurdle of all that separated them—one that, if it had not already been intact, Rachel would have mentally placed between them for her own sanity.

Because really, was there anything in this world quite as attractive as a cowboy daddy?

It took all day Saturday to disassemble the play set and saw the wood into pieces small enough to fit into woodstoves.

Seth felt great about the fact that he was doing double duty with his charity—working off the auction bid for the senior center and providing folks with wood to heat their homes through the winter cold—although right now, near the beginning of June, he was working up a good sweat under the sun's hot rays.

Seth had thought the project would take only a couple of weekends once the materials were delivered, but Rachel didn't want to work Sundays, and he respected that. And if he was being honest with himself, he wasn't exactly in a hurry to rush the job. He enjoyed hanging around Rachel, and Zooey and Caden really seemed to have hit it off, almost like an older sister with her baby brother. She had even offered to babysit while Seth and Rachel took the wood over to the community church for distribution.

As the sun started to disappear over the horizon, Seth and Rachel had finally loaded all the wood in the back of Seth's truck and had taken it to the church, where Pastor Shawn gave them a cheerful welcome.

"Good to see you, Seth," the pastor said, shaking Seth's hand before filling his arms with wood pieces. "Let's stack the wood on the south side and I'll put a tarp over it to keep it clean and dry until people need it."

While the three of them unloaded and piled the wood, Shawn and Rachel conversed easily with each other, catching up on the week's events and talking about who was ill, who'd been promoted and how excited Shawn was for the Vacation Bible School program this year.

Seth knew they didn't purposefully exclude him from the conversation, but that didn't stop him from feeling like the odd man out.

The third wheel.

He didn't know a lot about the pastor, since Shawn, who wasn't originally from Serendipity, had been received into the community church after Seth had enlisted in the army.

Shawn had officiated at Tracy's funeral, but Seth had been too full of grief, and too overwhelmed by his new role as Caden's guardian, to really pay much attention to him then.

It had never bothered Seth before that he usually skipped Sunday services. He knew his parents were probably disappointed that he didn't attend more often. They had diligently raised him and his sister, Samantha, in the Christian faith, and they rarely missed a Sunday themselves.

But he just wasn't ready.

Anyway, he had a full life and a busy schedule to keep—especially now that he was learning parenthood and ranching all at once. He didn't like feeling cooped up by four walls while he listened to a preacher drone on for half an hour.

God was everywhere, wasn't He? Seth didn't need to be caught up in a stained-glass-windowed establishment, sitting on a hard pew and using kneelers every Sunday morning, to pray and stuff.

Did he?

As Shawn and Rachel talked about various parishioners, Seth began to see what he was missing. It felt a little bit like what he heard when he visited Cup O' Jo's Café, which was the best place in town to catch up on all the latest goings-on.

Everybody knew everybody here, and Jo Spencer, the queen bee of the gossip hive from her prime position as proprietor and waitress in the café named after her, had the lowdown on everyone and loved to share it. She considered herself most folks' second mother,

Seth included, and she always made people feel like they were at home.

He knew all the people Shawn and Rachel were discussing—Serendipity was a small town with one Main Street and a single three-way stoplight.

This felt different, though.

Not gossip. Not news.

Something deeper.

It wasn't just what was happening and to whom, but who was going through current trials and how they could help people get back on their feet. He listened as they planned to provide meals to the sick or transportation for the housebound. Visit shut-ins and those laid up in the hospital.

Practical, useful stuff.

Though it had originally been his idea to give away the planks from the playhouse to use as firewood, Rachel's suggestion to donate the lot to the chapel to help parishioners stay warm seemed to fit right into the church's mission. It was summer now, but it wouldn't be long before the nights became cooler and fall approached, and it was good to plan ahead for how to help.

This was community.

And Seth, who'd been born and raised here, suddenly felt like somehow he was missing out.

Which made him even more uncomfortable. The sooner they got the wood unloaded and got out of there, the better.

Just as Seth was grabbing the last of the wood and stacking it against the side of the church, the pastor clapped him on the shoulder.

"This is a good thing you're doing here," he said, opening a tarp he'd brought out to cover the pile.

"Bringing the wood in, you mean?"

"Helping Rachel."

Seth barked out a laugh. "She bought me at the Bachelors and Baskets Auction. I'm working off my time by building a new play set for her day care."

"That's not the way I heard it."

Shawn chuckled. "No?"

"It sounds like there's been a lot of upheaval in your life recently. Tracy's death. Accepting Caden's guardianship. It says a lot about a man that he fulfills his obligations even under duress."

"I wouldn't call it duress." Seth frowned. He wasn't caring for Caden under any kind of compulsion. Caden wasn't just his responsibility—he was his family now.

He shrugged but didn't elaborate. Was this going to be the beginning of a sermon? He hoped not. That was the last thing he needed right now.

"Rachel said she tried to absolve you of your obligation to her, but you refused."

Again, Seth shrugged. "I'm not the kind of man to renege on a promise. Besides, I like to build things. It's kind of a hobby for me."

Shawn nodded, his gaze full of respect. "So you're building something as intricate as a play set, even though you've suddenly found yourself the adoptive father of a baby and have a ranch to run. That can't be easy."

"The gossip hive must be buzzing overtime," Seth muttered irritably, stooping to rearrange the woodpile rather than continuing to make eye contact with the pastor.

"People are concerned about you and Caden, and they want to help," Rachel said, laying a reassuring hand on his arm. He hadn't heard her come up beside him and her touch was like a zap of electricity bolting through him.

"No one needs to worry about me. I'm handling it."

He didn't know why he'd said that, especially with a resentful tone to his voice that even he could discern.

For one thing, Rachel knew exactly how well he was *not* handling it. And for another, even he could see that he was letting his pride and male ego get in his way.

For Caden's sake, he needed to take all the help he could get and be grateful for it. But it wouldn't be easy. He wasn't good at being humble. He didn't like accepting things when he'd rather be giving them.

And he especially wasn't thrilled about the idea of all of the people in church watching him and finding him wanting in any way.

Were they *concerned* that he wouldn't be good enough for Caden? Did they think the baby deserved better?

He could hardly blame them if they did. There wasn't a moment that had passed since he'd been given the guardianship of Caden that he hadn't wondered the same thing himself. He'd measured himself often—had he come up wanting?

Where had the stubborn streak suddenly come from? If he looked foolish, it was no one's fault but his own.

"I appreciate your concern," he said, relaxing his shoulders as he allowed his resentment and stubborn ego to flow out of him.

"As Rachel well knows, raising a baby on your own is no easy task," Pastor Shawn said. "But when it comes at you with no warning— Well, I remember how difficult the first few weeks were."

Pastor Shawn *remembered*? What did that mean?

"You have a baby?"

Shawn nodded. "A little girl. Noelle. She was abandoned in my church on Christmas Eve a year and a half ago. I found her tucked into the hay in the manger the kids used for the Christmas pageant. I was just getting ready to leave after the late service when I heard a strange sound. You can imagine my surprise when I found a live baby in the manger."

Seth was stunned. As unusual as his situation was, it wasn't completely unheard of for someone to gain custody of a godchild if something happened to the parents, and he'd given Luke and Tracy his consent when they were amending their will, so it wasn't as if he'd never considered the possibility. He'd just never thought it would happen.

Shawn's circumstances beat his by miles.

What a story.

"I kept her at my place for the weekend due to it being the Christmas holidays and all. And then…well, I just plain fell in love with the sweet little thing."

"So you adopted her?" Seth asked, running a hand across his jaw.

Shawn laughed. "It wasn't quite that simple, but eventually, yes. First I applied to be her foster father. Even that is a pretty far stretch from the norm—a single man wanting to foster a baby girl. I probably wouldn't have been able to keep her were it not for Heather. She had three foster kids of her own, so she knew how the system worked. She guided me through it from start to finish or I would never have made it. *And* she knew all about child care, which I think was my biggest learning curve. Dirty diapers." He grinned and shivered dramatically.

Seth groaned. He had a learning curve not only with Caden—and dirty diapers—but also with the Bar H ranch. At least Luke and Tracy's will clearly stated that he was Caden's legal guardian, so he didn't have to worry about someone trying to take him away.

When the time came, which would be as soon as he was able to file the papers, he'd fully adopt Caden as his son.

No question about it.

"I thank God every day that he brought Heather, her children and baby Noelle into my life. They are my biggest blessings and have filled my world with joy."

He clapped Seth on the back. "Let me give you some advice, son. Not as a pastor, but as a man. You hold on tight to this one," Shawn said, nodding toward Rachel. "You'll find she'll be an invaluable resource to you, just as Heather was, and is, to me."

Rachel's face reddened under the pastor's praise, but this was one situation where Seth agreed with Shawn. After his family, Rachel had been the first person Seth had turned to after he had become Caden's legal guardian. And what had started as a desperate cry for help had only grown from there. It seemed he and Rachel were spending more and more time together, and he wasn't about to complain.

When he had questions about Caden's care—which was often—she had answers. She'd encouraged him to call at any time of day or night. And sometimes he did.

But it was more than just getting answers to the billions of issues that cropped up.

It was Rachel's own brand of *encouragement* that

she gave him—which was probably what he needed most of all right now.

"Oh, I'm not letting her go anywhere," Seth assured Shawn. "Believe me, I know what a blessing I have in her, and in her daughter, Zooey, who is babysitting Caden as we speak. I'm probably driving Rachel crazy with all my questions and concerns, but she has unending patience."

"No, not at all." Rachel didn't waste a moment in responding. "You're not a bother."

"I felt the same way about Heather. I figured with the way I was hounding her, I would chase her away. Thankfully, she doesn't scare easily. I still have new questions all the time, even though Noelle is now a toddler like Caden. I guess we both ought to be thankful that the Lord made ladies of sterner stuff than us, huh?"

"You're still friends with Heather?" For some reason the answer to that question was inordinately important to Seth and he held his breath waiting for the answer.

"Oh, yes. Best friends." Shawn grinned.

Rachel sputtered.

Seth looked from Shawn to Rachel and back again, feeling like he'd missed something important.

"We are best friends," Shawn repeated. "And so much more than that. I was slow at figuring out my emotions at first, but I'm no fool. I made that woman my wife."

If a smile on a man of God could be called wily, then that was absolutely the right adjective for Shawn's toothy grin, and it was followed by a knowing wink in Rachel's direction, making Seth's skin itch all over.

A pastor winking at one of his parishioners. Wasn't there a rule against that?

"You never know about these things," Shawn continued. "The right people come into your life when you least expect it. As they say, the Lord works in mysterious ways."

Chapter Five

Rachel didn't know who *they* were—the ones who were spouting off nonsense about the Lord working in mysterious ways. If it was in the Bible, Rachel didn't know where, but then again, the proverb had come from Pastor Shawn's lips, and he was definitely the one who would have the most insight on the ins and outs of the way the Lord worked, wasn't he?

She was certainly no expert, despite that she read her Bible, prayed daily and went to Sunday services. Her faith had rescued her many a time, and yet she made no bones of the fact that she didn't always understand why things happened the way they did. She just held on to faith that the Lord had it all in hand.

But in this instance the pastor was mistaken. However the Lord was working, mysterious or otherwise, He was not interested in the romantic prospects of Seth and Rachel as a couple. They both had far too much on their plates to so much as consider a relationship with each other. Put it together and there would be an enormous explosion—and that was without the dozens of reasons she'd given Zooey and Lizzie for why such a relationship could not and would not ever exist.

Though if there was one really good thing to come out of this whirlwind of change—besides sweet Caden—it was that Zooey's attitude had appeared to have calmed down a bit. She'd attended summer school that week without a single protest, and on time, and had completed all her homework without having to be nagged—er, *reminded*.

She'd even offered to accompany Rachel to Seth's ranch so she could play with Caden while Rachel figured out the bookkeeping software with Seth at the end of the next week. After moving into the Bar H ranch house, Seth had spent his evenings during the week building her new play set, and she was anxious to return the favor.

When they arrived at the ranch, it was to find a beaming Seth bouncing on his toes with excitement as Caden toddled around the paddock area.

Curious. Smiling and abounding with energy wasn't quite the reception Rachel had been anticipating from Seth, given his aversion to all things numerical.

"Watch this," Seth exclaimed as soon as Rachel and Zooey had exited her sedan. "Come here, Caden, and show Zooey and Miss Rachel what you can do."

Caden giggled and immediately responded to Seth's open arms, reaching his chubby little hands up to grasp Seth's thumbs.

"Prepare to be amazed."

Seth's grin widened even more, if that was possible, and Rachel couldn't help but smile herself.

"All right, little man, let's show off your trick for the ladies."

Seth crouched slightly, and with his encouragement, Caden stepped one foot onto Seth's knee, then the other, and as Seth slowly straightened, Caden continued to walk up his body. Seth remained steady with a good grip on the toddler's hands as the little guy's feet stepped on his chest.

Then, with a delighted squeal, Caden pushed off and flipped backward. With a whoop of excitement of his own, Seth skillfully set Caden on his feet for a perfect landing.

"Again. Again," Caden pleaded.

"Is that not the most incredible thing you've ever seen?" Seth crowed, scrubbing an affectionate hand through Caden's hair.

Rachel didn't know whether to be appalled or impressed. She was a little of both, she supposed. Two years old was a little young for backflips, in her opinion, but Seth had him completely under control every movement of the execution. Most interesting of all, Seth appeared just as excited about what Caden had done as if he and the boy were blood relatives.

And from what she'd just seen Caden do, they almost might have been.

"Awesomesauce," she said, clapping.

Zooey groaned. "Mo-om," she wailed, stretching out the word. "No one says *awesomesauce* anymore."

"'Sauce," Caden repeated, jumping and grinning and patting his tummy.

"Caden does. See?" Rachel laughed. "I have been vindicated—by a two-year-old."

Seth chuckled. "Not to burst your bubble or anything, but I'm pretty sure Caden thinks you were referring to *applesauce*, which is one of his favorite foods."

Zooey snorted and Rachel narrowed her eyes on her and pursed her lips.

"Just go ahead and laugh at your mother, Miss Too-Cool-for-Words."

Zooey's eyes twinkled and she pressed her lips together, but a giggle escaped her nonetheless.

"Looks like you're one proud papa, with what Caden just did," Rachel said, shifting her attention to Seth and away from her rascally daughter.

"Right?" He pumped his fist in the air. "Two years old and I have just taught him his first parkour trick. He may have set a world record or something."

"I don't know about a world record, but definitely like father, like son," she agreed.

His smile wavered. "That still sounds so strange to me. I mean, there's no question that I'm going to legally adopt him, or that I am a proud parent. But do you think I'll ever get used to being called Daddy?"

"It'll take a while. Most parents have nine months to prepare themselves to be called Mommy or Daddy, and it still sounds odd at first, even after the baby is born. Don't worry about it, though. After a while it'll sound natural."

"Can you teach me some of those moves, like you did with Caden?" Zooey asked, excitement crackling in the tone of her voice.

Zooey wanted to learn parkour?

What was that about?

"You are much too tall to walk up Seth's chest and do a backflip," Rachel pointed out, thinking that was the end of that.

"Well, no," Seth concurred. "It won't work that way. But if you're up for it, I think I can teach you how to take a running start at a hay bale, then bank off it and do a pretty nifty backflip."

"Cool beans," Zooey exclaimed.

"Oh, I see. So it's okay for you to say *cool beans*, but *awesomesauce* is out of the question?"

"'Sauce," Caden repeated.

"I think he's hungry," said Seth, and the three of them laughed over it. "I'll give him a snack while we work on the computer."

"Which we probably ought to be doing right now," Rachel said, hoping all this nonsense about Zooey attempting parkour moves would blow over. Rachel had never known Zooey to be the least bit interested in athletic endeavors in the past. She regularly complained about the running she had to do in gym class. Since Zooey was healthy and got plenty of activity walking around town, Rachel had never kicked up a fuss about trying to get her involved in sports.

She certainly never would have expected her daughter to sound so enthusiastic about parkour. If she had to have a sudden athletic interest, couldn't she have gotten fired up about swim team? Or soccer? Or something else that seemed less likely to end in a broken neck?

Rachel wished they could skip the parkour and go straight to the software.

But given the circumstances, she preferred to spar with her daughter over expressions like *awesomesauce* and *cool beans* than ponder the disaster that was no doubt coming next.

"It'll only take a moment for me to show Zooey the move," Seth said. "Ready, Zooey?"

Zooey nodded eagerly.

Rachel scooped Caden into her arms and patted his back, reassuring herself as much as him.

"You're going to approach the hay bale at a jog," Seth explained. "Then you're going to plant your feet against the top edge of the bale and push yourself upward and backward. Like this."

He demonstrated, making the entire move look fluid and ridiculously simple.

Rachel knew what would happen were *she* to try such a trick. She'd trip right over the hay bale and take a nosedive that would leave her scratched up for weeks. And that was to say nothing of her dignity.

She only hoped her daughter would be able to keep *her* dignity intact—along with all of her bones. That backflip looked like it could go wrong all too easily.

"Ready to try it?" he asked Zooey. "Don't worry. I'll be right here to spot you."

Rachel kissed Caden's soft cheek and whispered, "If you ask me, this is a very bad idea. Don't tell your daddy, though. I wouldn't want him to think I'm not supporting him."

She held her breath as Zooey broke into a jog, her jaw set with determination. It looked as if she was going to successfully bank the hay bale, but at the last moment she tensed and skidded to a halt just short of it.

"Sorry," she murmured, looking crestfallen.

"No problem," Seth reassured her. "Sometimes it takes me many tries before I finally get a move right. Do you want to give it another go?"

No, she does not, Rachel thought.

But Zooey said, "Yeah. I think I just psyched myself out there for a moment. I can do this."

"It's all in your mind," Seth said. "If you believe you

can do it, your body will follow your mind's lead, even if you have to work on it. You'll find that after a while, flipping is the easy part."

Rachel couldn't have disagreed more. Doing a backflip by banking off a hay bale was most definitely not something one did all in one's head, but before Rachel could voice her concerns, Zooey was already racing toward the hay bale.

With a whoop, she planted her feet right where Seth had indicated and, with just the slightest bit of assistance on Seth's part in order to help her to get all the way over, she completed a backflip and landed on her feet.

"I did it. Did you see that, Mom? Woo-hoo!"

Zooey's whole body was pulsing with energy and her expression was a match for how she used to look on Christmas mornings when she was a tiny tot.

"That was great, honey."

Rachel relaxed some after she'd observed the careful way Seth had confidently and knowledgeably spotted her daughter through the entire flip.

There was no way Zooey could have fallen. Not in Seth's capable hands.

"Can we do it again?" Zooey's enthusiasm was catching, and Rachel even caught herself smiling. Caden had been asking the very same thing only minutes earlier.

"One more time, and then Seth and I need to work on the ranch's books."

"Parkour's more fun," Seth muttered under his breath, frowning like a little boy who'd just had his favorite toy taken away from him.

"That may well be," Rachel said, though she didn't

exactly agree. "But sometimes we've got no choice except to *adult*, like it or not."

Seth screwed up his face at Zooey and cringed like he'd just sucked a lemon. "Take my advice and don't grow up."

Zooey laughed, as did Rachel. She was amazed by the way Seth so effortlessly appeared to reach her daughter.

Seth spotted Zooey through a second banking backflip. Rachel couldn't help but be impressed. He had a gift, not only of performing parkour himself but of teaching it to a two-year-old and a sixteen-year-old.

As she well knew, not everyone was good at working with children, especially over such an expansive age range.

She was surprised at how vigorously Zooey was taking to the sport. Now she was talking about backflips and learning how to walk up walls and leap benches in a single bound, superhero-style. Strange words coming from a teenager who'd never before been remotely interested in gymnastics, dance or even running.

"Back to being a cowboy," Seth said with a sigh. "Putting on my big-boy hat now."

He sounded miserable, and the joy that had lit his face only moments before was doused out.

"If it's any consolation, you look fantastic in a cowboy hat."

As soon as the words were out of her mouth, heat rushed to her face. She sounded as if she was flirting with him.

Which she wasn't.

Much.

He straightened and his smile returned. Maybe the compliment *had* done him some good.

"I got one for Caden, too. A white hat, 'cause he's one of the good guys. And boots so he really looks the part. He's already a serious lady-killer. Those little girls in your day care had better watch out or he'll knock their socks right off their feet."

Rachel grinned. That much was true.

"Like father, like son."

Seth led everyone into Tracy's old office, which was little more than an offshoot built onto one side of the stable. The front room held a desk with an ancient computer monitor. The back room contained the printer and a couple of metal filing cabinets. Zooey laid down a blanket for Caden in the back room and pulled a few books out of her backpack to read to him.

"Here's Tracy's old work computer."

The smell of old leather and fresh horse assaulted his nostrils, as it did every time he entered the stable. He was slowly getting used to it.

Old tack, mostly bridles and neck yokes used for pulling wagons, decorated one wall, featuring an antique wooden wagon wheel as a centerpiece. The opposite wall sported a large display of spurs, some polished to a high shine and others rusty with wear. Seth suspected some of them might even go back a hundred years or more.

There was some serious history in this building.

Including the computer.

The monitor was a gigantic box type that reminded Seth of an old-time television set. Seriously. How long ago had the flat screen been invented?

Apparently, Luke and Tracy hadn't been interested in upgrading to anything made in this century.

"Do you see what I'm working with here?" he complained. "I know how to use a computer, obviously, and I enjoy playing games on my console—but this? This is one intimidating piece of software."

"Hardware, actually. The software is the program we'll use to help with the accounting."

His face heated. He was a soldier. He didn't like exposing his weaknesses.

"But this monitor?" she said, smiling to cover his faux pas. "Yes, it's a dinosaur, all right."

"Yeah. A T. rex."

"Let's conquer this thing, shall we?"

He pulled back the office chair for her, then pushed a second chair up beside her. She turned on the computer and the monitor snapped and crackled to life.

"Fortunately, it looks like the CPU itself is a relatively new model," she explained, "one that can easily host an up-to-date accounting software."

"And that's a good thing?"

"That's a great thing." She held up the finance CD lying on the desktop and waved it at him. "I use this very same program with my day care. This little guy here is going to make your life considerably easier."

"I hope so," he muttered, but didn't really believe it would help him much.

Any math was too much math in his book.

Rachel sifted through the piles of invoices, separating those that had been paid from those yet due, as well as taking a quick gander at the bookkeeping program's spreadsheets to look at the accounts payable and receivable, as well as the payroll.

"Since the printer has a scanning feature, we'll start by scanning all of these documents into the computer. The software will automatically sort your receipts into categories, and by the time we're finished, we'll have most of the documents you'll need to give your tax accountant—profit and loss, balance sheets and detailed lists of receivables and payables."

"What I've learned so far is that ranching is a long game. Cows are bred in the spring and fall and delivered eight months later. When the calves get weaned, we sell them. The rest of the year we're working with that profit."

Even though he'd managed to learn that much, Seth's head was still spinning. As a soldier, he'd been kept comfortably fed and bedded, or as much as possible for a man on tour to the Middle East. He hadn't had much reason, or opportunity, to use the money he was accruing, so most of what he'd made had gone straight into his savings accounts. He wouldn't know a financial balance sheet if it bit him in the nose.

Rachel was staring at him curiously. "You look green around the gills."

Great. Wonderful. So he looked as bad as he felt.

And of course Rachel had noticed.

"I'm good." He straightened his shoulders and made direct eye contact with her. His stomach might be lurching, but that was his business and his alone.

"Like I said, the software does most of the work for you. Once you get familiar with the categories Luke and Tracy set up to run the ranch, the bookkeeping shouldn't take much more than a couple of hours a week, max."

"That's better than the entire day I spent last Wednesday. As you can see, I didn't make a dent in it at all. The only thing I got was a headache."

Her head tilted in concern as she observed him. "You don't have to learn this. You could hire someone to come in and keep the books for you."

Seth shook his head. "No way. Tracy always did this on her own. She said it was the best way to know what was really going on with the ranch. I'm not going to pass that baton just because it's a little confusing. If I'm going to do this thing, I'm in it for all or nothing."

"Good for you." She laid a hand on his shoulder and smiled up at him. "You're just psyching yourself out. It's like you said to Zooey about parkour. Accounting is really not as hard as it looks. You'll get the hang of it. Most of what's holding you back is in your mind."

"Yeah, but I've never been good at math."

He was itching in discomfort. She must think he was a dumb jock, able to swing through trees but not add two plus two together.

Her gaze met his, and to his amazement, he didn't see a trace of ridicule or disdain in its depths. Only encouragement and reassurance.

"Keep in mind that Zooey has never done a backflip in her life. Yet with your help, she did it today. Twice. Think of this software as your backflip. I'm going to help you get through it."

Seth lowered his brow in concentration. "You're saying I need to explore new ways to see the obstacles in my world."

"Precisely. Now, as I was saying, one very nice feature of this particular software is its ability to read and organize scanned documents. Back before the advent of the computer, everything had to be written into paper ledgers. When computers came on the scene, those numbers could be manually entered into an accounting software program. That was definitely less of a hassle than scribbling on paper and easier to keep organized, but it still took a fairly significant amount of time. Now we just stack—" she demonstrated by straightening the pile of invoices in front of her "—and scan. The software sorts and categorizes line items into categories for you."

"Awesomesauce," Seth said drily. "Which reminds me. I'm getting hungry. I have veggies all cut up and ready to eat back at the ranch house. Aren't you ready for a snack?"

"No, and neither are you, at least until you get a feel for the categories Luke and Tracy used. Stop dangling carrots in front of me," she teased. "Now, if we also take a quick look at how they had their personal accounts organized, we will have a clearer picture of what was important to them, both in the short-term and in the long-term. You'll be able to discover not only how they wanted their ranch to be run but also what they considered the most important investments.

"You can see here where they set aside the money for Caden's college trust fund and how they funneled money into it on a regular basis. And hey, look here."

Rachel sounded excited, and Seth leaned in over her shoulder, his palm on the desk next to hers, so he could see what she was pointing at.

A sweet scent wafted across his senses, clouding his mind. It was her shampoo, he realized, and it smelled a great deal better than the office around them.

Coconut.

He liked coconut.

It was all he could do not to lean in closer, just to get another whiff.

"See here?" She pointed at a line item.

"'Caden's horse.'" Seth's throat tightened and he had to clear it in order to speak. "They were saving to buy him his first horse."

"Looks like."

"But why? There are more than a half-dozen horses in the stable already."

"Yes, but they're used by the wranglers who work your cattle, aren't they? Did any of them even belong to Luke and Tracy? And even if some of them do, Caden's horse would have to be especially gentle when he was first learning to ride. Maybe they were looking for something special, just for him."

Seth shrugged. She had a point. He lifted his hat by the crown and tossed it onto the side of the desk, then jammed his fingers through the thick ends of his hair, which was only just beginning to grow out to where he liked it, now that he was no longer in the military.

He blew out a breath. It seemed like every time he turned around, he found out something else he didn't know, and he was getting weary of it.

"I haven't been able to work all that out yet," he admitted. "The horses, the cattle. Pigs. Chickens. I really don't know what I'm supposed to do with it all. I do know that at least a couple of the horses stabled now are—*were*—Luke and Tracy's personal mounts. I've been riding Luke's horse, Windsong. I'll have to check on the rest, whether the ranch owns them or if they are the wranglers' personal mounts."

"We can get those details later. I think for right now it's enough to be aware that the Hollisters wanted Caden to have a horse in his future. Maybe somewhere around his third birthday next month. Unless you'd rather start looking now."

"Isn't Caden a little young for a horse?"

Rachel laughed. "I'm no expert, of course, having never ridden myself, but Caden is likely to grow up to be a rancher, after all, since this land is his legacy. I think most of the children in Serendipity start out riding fairly young."

"I'll ask Wes," he said, referring to the ranch manager who'd been patiently walking him through all the many facets of owning a ranch. "He'll know when will be the right time for us to start looking for a gentle horse, and more important, where to find one, because I haven't got a clue."

"That sounds like a reasonable plan."

He felt as if his head was going to burst.

"Would it be too much for me to ask you to accompany me when the time comes?"

Her beautiful brown eyes widened. "I'd be happy to go with you, but I don't know what kind of help I can give you. I know less about horses than you do."

"True, you may not know anything about horses, but you do know children. I think you'd be better able to recognize a bond between Caden and his potential horse than I would."

That was the rational reason, if a little flimsy, and it was the only one he was going to admit to.

"Do you mind if I make a suggestion?" She turned slightly in her chair so she was looking up at him and she rested her palm over the top of his hand on the desk.

Her expression exuded empathy and her touch somehow calmed him as much as her gaze did. The tension in his shoulders eased and the pounding in his head decreased until it was down to a dull roar.

"Please do."

"Start making lists of things you plan to do. Write stuff down. Don't try to keep it all straight in your head. There's too much for you to remember and you're getting overwhelmed."

"I'm way past overwhelmed. But I have been making lists."

She smiled softly and tapped his temple with the tip of her finger. "Yes, I know. Up here, right?"

Was that why his head always felt ready to explode?

"Use your cell phone. I've got a good app I can show you how to use. You can divide your projects into categories so you don't forget anything and tick items off as you go."

"And psychologically make myself feel as if I'm accomplishing something."

"Exactly." She grinned, and he chuckled.

He'd had enough of standing and staring at numbers. He wanted to climb on something, stretch his back and legs and work out the kinks in his muscles.

But because he was stuck in a musty old office that smelled of horsehair and leather, he did the next best thing.

He reached for Rachel's hands, drew her to her feet and twirled her around until they were both laughing and out of breath.

"What would I do without you?" he asked, hoping he never had to find out. At least, not for a long time to come. At the moment he couldn't imagine being able to conquer all those *lists* without her. She was his number one go-to person where Caden was concerned. "You've got my six, and I really appreciate it."

She squeezed his hands.

"No worries there. I'll be around to help you as long as you need me."

She winked and Seth's breath caught in his throat.

He'd known Rachel long enough to be sure she wasn't the flirtatious type, and they'd both established that they weren't in the market for a relationship.

But right this second, he couldn't seem to remember any of the reasons why. She touched his heart in a way no other woman ever had.

Granted, he hadn't had many relationships in his adult life, since he'd enlisted in the army straight out of high school and had served two tours overseas. He wasn't sure if he'd know true feelings if he tripped over them.

But this thing with Rachel? It felt real.

She must have read his thoughts in his expression. Her face pinkened and she pulled her hands away.

He cleared his throat. "We…uh…probably ought to go check on Zooey and Caden. They must be getting hungry for a snack. I know I am."

"Sure," Rachel agreed, her eyes glowing. She'd recovered quicker than he had. He couldn't even tell she'd been flustered only moments earlier. "I'll let you off the hook this time. But next time we're going to go over your balance sheet."

One more reason to like her. She knew when to push him and when to back off, and she wasn't afraid to do either.

He suspected they would be friends long after he'd

straightened out this mess with the ranch, and even when he was more confident in raising Caden.

As if she guessed what he was thinking, she grabbed his cowboy hat from the edge of the desk and reached on tiptoe to plant it on his head, tilting her chin and appraising him before giving the brim of his hat a little tug.

"There," she said, sounding pleased with herself. "You have the looks, and soon you'll have the know-how. We'll make a cowboy out of you yet."

Chapter Six

Exactly one week and one day later, Rachel sifted through her blouses on the hangers in her closet, looking for the perfect shirt for the day ahead. Ultimately, she settled on a soft-pink cotton pullover. She needed something to match her oldest pair of jeans and the brand-spanking-new pair of burgundy-colored riding boots she'd purchased from Emerson's Hardware earlier in the week.

She had no intention whatsoever of actually riding a horse, but since she was spending an increasing amount of time on the Bar H ranch with Seth, it only made sense to dress like the ranchers did. She didn't want to ruin her good running shoes trudging through mud and cow pies.

So now she had a pair of riding boots she'd never use to ride a horse and a pair of running shoes that would never see so much as a single run.

Irony was her middle name.

"I'm going out," she told Zooey, who was lying across the couch with her feet propped up higher than her head, chatting away on her cell phone to one of her friends about a new boy in town named Dawson.

Rachel wasn't trying to eavesdrop, exactly, but it was hard to miss Zooey's excited giggle when she exclaimed how cute he was and asked her friend if he would be at the party.

Typical teenage conversation.

Nothing to be concerned about. As much as she wanted to put a large rock on Zooey's head to keep her from growing up, it was happening whether she liked it or not.

In two years Zooey would be off to college and Rachel would still be here. Only, in the evenings, the house would be too quiet.

She would be alone.

If she didn't think about it, would it go away?

She wished that she had more time, that she could do it all over again. But this was the way the Lord had made the relationship between parents and their children. Parents nurtured their kids into adulthood. And the older the kids got, the less they needed their moms.

Or in Seth's case, dad. In some ways she envied Seth, being able to cuddle little Caden in his arms whenever he wanted to, having so many more years ahead of them before Caden, too, was grown and gone.

Zooey was long past the cuddling stage. Once in a great while she still wanted or needed a hug from her mom, but that was happening less often, especially after she'd started hanging out with that questionable group of friends.

She'd been doing better for the past few weeks, putting effort into summer school and spending more time playing with Caden than she did out by the pool.

Rachel wondered if that was one of those friends she was speaking to now. And what was that about a party?

Rachel waved to get Zooey's attention and indicated for her to put the phone on mute. Instead, she surprised Rachel by telling her friend she'd talk to her later and hanging up, giving Rachel her full attention.

"Seth's picking me up in a minute. We're going out to the McKenna ranch to see about getting Caden a horse. According to Seth's foreman, the earlier a future rancher learns to ride, the better. Make sure you get your homework done. You know I don't like it if you have to study on a Sunday."

"Yeah. I know. I finished my homework last night. Can I come along with you to see the horses?"

"I'll have to ask Seth, but I don't see why not. We can probably use the help with Caden."

"Awesomesauce," Zooey replied, flashing Rachel a sassy grin.

"It's not that bad."

"No," Zooey agreed. "In fact, I think it will go viral. I'll make a video. 'Moms Using Out-of-Date Vernacular.' Pretty soon everybody's mom will want to make a video and upload it online."

"Hey, watch yourself, Miss Cool Beans." She gestured toward the phone. "Who was that, by the way?"

"Just Abby."

"Abby? I don't think I've heard that name before."

"You should have. Abigail Carter. She's in my class at school, and she was in your day care when she was a toddler. We used to play in the sandbox together."

"Oh, that Abby. I know you used to be friends, way back when, but I haven't heard her name mentioned in years. What happened?"

"I dunno. Different paths, different interests. But we've kind of reconnected lately."

"Over *Dawson*?" Rachel was only half teasing.

Zooey's face turned a vibrant red and she rolled to her feet.

"*Mom*," she wailed. "My phone conversations are supposed to be private."

"Can I help it if you talk loud? I could hear you all the way down the hallway in my bedroom. I would have had to shut my door and put in earplugs not to hear every word you said."

"Please, please don't embarrass me by mentioning this to anyone?"

Rachel flashed an impish smile. "Why would I do that?"

She wouldn't, of course, but it was too funny to see Zooey squirm.

"What party, by the way?"

"Mom," Zooey protested again.

"Will there be an adult chaperone? I'd like a phone number so I can check out the details."

Zooey crossed her arms and frowned. "Check up on me, you mean."

"I'm just doing what any responsible parent would do. It's not that I don't trust you, but I do want you to be safe. So sue me."

She did trust Zooey, although in recent months, that trust had been sorely tested.

"But there's no reason not to share that information with me, right? If everything is on the up-and-up, which I'm sure it is, and you've got nothing to hide, then there should be no problem."

"There is no problem." Zooey rolled her eyes and sighed. "If you insist. The chaperone's name is Pas-

YOUR FAVORITE INSPIRATIONAL NOVELS!

GET 2 FREE BOOKS!

2 FREE BOOKS

To get your 2 free books, affix this peel-off sticker to the reply card and mail it today!

Plus, receive
TWO FREE BONUS GIFTS!

We'd like to send you two free books from the series you are enjoying now. Your two books have a combined cover price of over $10 retail, but are yours to keep absolutely FREE! We'll even send you two wonderful surprise gifts. You can't lose!

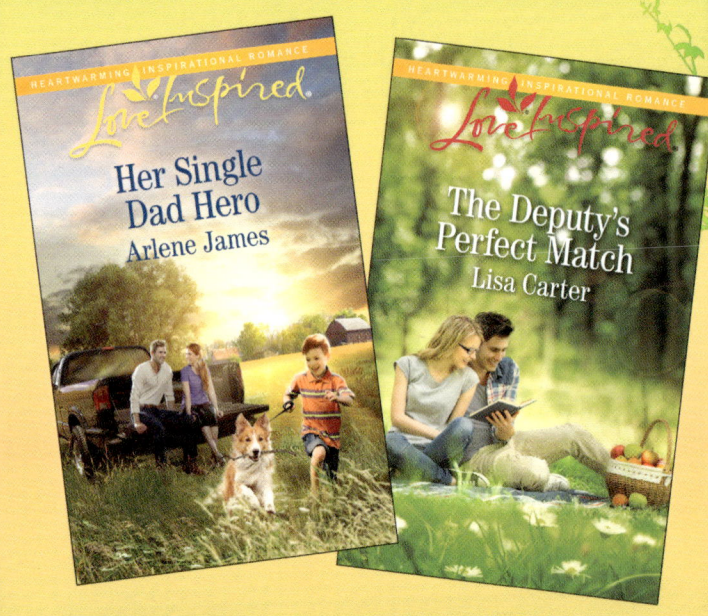

Each of your FREE books features unique characters, interesting settings and captivating stories you won't want to miss!

FREE BONUS GIFTS!

We'll send you two wonderful surprise gifts, worth about $10 retail, **absolutely FREE**, just for giving our books a try! Don't miss out — MAIL THE REPLY CARD TODAY!

Visit us at
www.ReaderService.com

Books received may not be as shown.

GET 2 FREE BOOKS!

CLAIM NOW!
Return this card today to get 2 FREE Books and 2 FREE Bonus Gifts!

▶ DETACH AND MAIL CARD TODAY! ▶

YES! Please send me the **2 FREE books** and **2 FREE bonus gifts** for which I qualify. I understand that I am under no obligation to purchase anything further, as explained on the back of this card.

PLACE FREE GIFTS SEAL HERE

❏ I prefer the regular-print edition
105/305 IDL GLUR

❏ I prefer the larger-print edition
122/322 IDL GLUR

FIRST NAME

LAST NAME

ADDRESS

APT.#

CITY

STATE/PROV.

ZIP/POSTAL CODE

Offer limited to one per household and not applicable to series that subscriber is currently receiving.
Your Privacy—The Reader Service is committed to protecting your privacy. Our Privacy Policy is available online at www.ReaderService.com or upon request from the Reader Service. We make a portion of our mailing list available to reputable third parties that offer products we believe may interest you. If you prefer that we not exchange your name with third parties, or if you wish to clarify or modify your communication preferences, please visit us at www.ReaderService.com/consumerschoice or write to us at Reader Service Preference Service, P.O. Box 9062, Buffalo, NY 14240-9062. Include your complete name and address.

® and ™ are trademarks owned and used by the trademark owner and/or its licensee. © 2016 HARLEQUIN ENTERPRISES LIMITED. Printed in the U.S.A.

LI-517-FMIVY17

READER SERVICE—Here's how it works:

Accepting your 2 free Love Inspired® Romance books and 2 free gifts (gifts valued at approximately $10.00 retail) places you under no obligation to buy anything. You may keep the books and gifts and return the shipping statement marked "cancel." If you do not cancel, about a month later we'll send you 6 additional books and bill you just $5.24 for the regular-print edition or $5.74 each for the larger-print edition in the U.S. or $5.74 each for the regular-print edition or $6.24 each for the larger-print edition in Canada. That is a savings of at least 13% off the cover price. It's quite a bargain! Shipping and handling is just 50¢ per book in the U.S. and 75¢ per book in Canada.* You may cancel at any time, but if you choose to continue, every month we'll send you 6 more books, which you may either purchase at the discount price plus shipping and handling or return to us and cancel your subscription. *Terms and prices subject to change without notice. Prices do not include applicable taxes. Sales tax applicable in N.Y. Canadian residents will be charged applicable taxes. Offer not valid in Quebec. Books received may not be as shown. All orders subject to approval. Credit or debit balances in a customer's account(s) may be offset by any other outstanding balance owed by or to the customer. Please allow 4 to 6 weeks for delivery. Offer available while quantities last.

▼ If offer card is missing write to: Reader Service, P.O. Box 1341, Buffalo, NY 14240-8531 or visit www.ReaderService.com ▼

BUSINESS REPLY MAIL
FIRST-CLASS MAIL   PERMIT NO. 717   BUFFALO, NY

POSTAGE WILL BE PAID BY ADDRESSEE

READER SERVICE
PO BOX 1341
BUFFALO NY 14240-8571

NO POSTAGE
NECESSARY
IF MAILED
IN THE
UNITED STATES

tor Shawn, and I'm fairly certain you already have the church's number stored on your cell phone."

"Pastor Shawn?" Rachel repeated, dumbfounded.

"The youth lock-in the weekend after next. I thought I'd go check it out. I thought maybe they were lame, but Abby says they're pretty fun." Zooey tried to make her voice sound casual, but Rachel could see right through the facade.

She wanted to jump for joy and pump her fists in the air. This was exactly what she'd been praying about for months. Zooey coming back to church? It was exactly the news she'd wanted to hear. And she definitely wanted Zooey to know she was pleased.

But fist pumping?

Somehow Rachel didn't think that would go over so well with her daughter.

Besides, there was one other thing.

"Don't take this the wrong way, honey. I'm thrilled that you're interested in attending a youth-group event, and I really like Abby, but I have to ask—does this sudden interest in youth group have anything to do with that Dawson boy?"

"No," Zooey exclaimed, the color in her face heightening once again. "Well, yes. I mean, he'll be there, but that's not why I'm going."

"Then why…?"

Zooey frowned and dropped her gaze, shoving her hands in the front pockets of her jeans. "I didn't want to have to tell you. I knew you'd be so ashamed of me for being so gullible. It's Lori and James. I found out they were getting into drugs." Her eyes filled with tears. "I can't believe I ever—"

Rachel opened her arms and Zooey ran into them.

She brushed the hair off her daughter's forehead and held her while she cried—for the loss of her friends, the loss of innocence and the vulnerability that had nearly landed Zooey in a situation beyond her control.

Rachel silently thanked God for taking care of her little girl.

Maybe Zooey no longer needed to snuggle like Caden, but in many ways a daughter would always need her mother, and right now, at this moment, holding Zooey and reassuring her that she would always be there for her was the most important thing in the world.

The sound of a truck's horn pulled them apart. Zooey sniffed and wiped her face on her sleeve, and Rachel found her eyes were also wet with tears. She reached for a tissue and dabbed at her eyelashes, hoping her mascara wouldn't leave any telltale signs that she'd been crying. She didn't want to embarrass Zooey by making this a public event.

"Shall I ask Seth if you can tag along?" Rachel asked, a little too brightly.

"Yeah. I'd like that."

Rachel dashed out to speak to Seth and returned a minute later with a broad smile on her face.

"Seth said he was hoping you'd want to come. He said he could use an extra opinion about which horse he should buy for Caden."

"He's probably just being nice to me because...well... I'm your daughter, and you know why he asked *you* to go, don't you?"

Zooey seemed to find something amusing in the question, for a reason Rachel didn't quite understand.

Rachel shot her a surprised look.

"Is this a trick question?"

"Do you think it's because you're such an expert on horses?" Zooey teased mercilessly. "I'm sure that's gotta be the reason."

"If you must know, he wants me to accompany him because I'm an expert on *children*. He thought I might have some insight and be able to discern whether Caden liked a particular horse or not."

"Good cover story."

"And what's that supposed to mean?" Rachel planted her fists on her hips and raised her eyebrows. "Be careful, missy. You're treading on thin ice here."

"All I'm saying," she said with a shrug that told Rachel she wasn't the least bit worried about her mother's threat, "is that if you can't figure out why Seth keeps asking you to do things with him, you're more hopeless than me."

"Seth and I are friends." Rachel didn't like the defensive note that had stolen into her voice.

Zooey just laughed.

"Right, Mom. You keep telling yourself that. I'll tell you this, though. Now that I'm hanging out with new peeps, I could sure use a 'friend' like that for myself."

The McKenna spread was much larger than the Bar H ranch. Two of the three McKenna brothers, along with their mother, Alice, still lived on the land. Alice lived in the main house, and Nick and Jax in separate cabins. Nick ran the cattle side of the operation, while Jax trained some of the finest horses around.

It was Jax they'd come to see. Wes had told Seth there was no one else like him in the county, maybe even the state. Jax knew horses like nobody's business, and if anyone could pick out the perfect horse for Caden, it was Jax.

Jax greeted the small gathering with a wave and a smile. He had already saddled three horses and had them hitched to the corral fence.

To Seth's untrained eye, he couldn't see why Jax would choose these animals over others. He had expected them to be smaller, for one thing, and maybe older. Preferably so old that the horse couldn't move beyond a walk if it had a bear chasing it.

That was Seth's idea of the perfect horse for Caden. But Jax was the expert, so he held his tongue.

"Oh, what beautiful horses," Rachel exclaimed, putting her hand in Seth's. He glanced down at her and she smiled, her eyes brimming with encouragement. Obviously, she'd seen the doubt he was feeling and wanted to reassure him.

He only hoped Jax wasn't as adept at reading faces. Seth didn't want Jax to think he was skeptical of him. Thankfully, Jax had turned to unhitch the first horse and lead him forward to introduce him to Seth and Caden.

"Now, let me start out by telling you that choosing horses for children isn't something I do a lot of. I usually train horses for ranch work or for the rodeo circuit and I've recently been working with some mustangs over at Faith Duggan's rescue ranch. I think I've got some good options for you, but I won't be offended if you want to look around at other places, get a sense of your options."

"Wes said there was no better man in the area when it came to evaluating horses," Seth said, a little surprised. He wasn't making *any* purchase until he was absolutely certain it was the right horse for Caden. "If Wes trusts you, then so do I."

"I appreciate that," Jax affirmed with a nod.

"These horses look big for such a little guy," Rachel said, verbally expressing the concern at the top of Seth's list. He squeezed her hand in gratitude and slowly released the breath he'd been holding.

Jax tipped back his hat and grinned. "Well, I figured you'd be wanting a horse Caden can grow with. You don't want his feet dragging the ground next time he has a growth spurt."

Seth chuckled, but it sounded dry even to his own ears. Caden gave a squeak of protest and wiggled in his arms and Seth realized he was holding him too tight. He made a conscious effort to relax his muscles.

Jax shifted his gaze to Seth. "Maybe you were expecting a pony?"

Seth didn't answer. He didn't want to look ill informed, especially not with Rachel standing right there. He'd been doing enough of that on his own lately without adding ponies to the list.

To his relief, Rachel spoke up. "I know I was. One of those cute little ones with the long manes. What are they called? Shetland ponies?"

Jax barked out a laugh. "Those 'cute little ones' are often the orneriest things you'll ever see. Trust me. You want a nice, steady quarter horse for Caden."

Seth did trust Jax, but when it came to his little Caden, a child who had already suffered so much in his short life, Seth was overprotective and not ashamed to admit it.

"Can I pet it?" Zooey asked, waiting for Jax's nod before running her hand down the dapple

"This is Monty. He's a seven-year-old gelding and as gentle as the day is long. Patient, too. You'll get a lot of good years out of him."

Rachel approached a palomino mare and stroked her muzzle.

"That's Fancy. She's a real sweetheart. Calm as can be. Very aware of her rider."

The third horse was a stunning black with four white socks and a sizzle of white lightning down his muzzle.

"We call that one Storm," Jax said as Seth approached and Caden reached out to tangle his fingers in the gelding's dark mane. "For obvious reasons. I'll admit it was probably not the most original name I've ever come up with."

"But it fits," said Seth, tracing his fingers along the white slash on the horse's face.

"In looks, yes," Jax agreed. "But in temperament, not so much. You'll never find a steadier, more tranquil horse than Storm here."

Caden was mesmerized by the black. Seth had been worried that Caden might get too excited and frighten the horses with his quick movements, but even when the toddler leaned over and hugged Storm's neck, the horse didn't so much as toss his head or skitter to the side. Instead, to Seth's amazement, Storm bowed his head toward the little boy. It almost looked like Caden was getting a horsey hug in return.

"It looks like we might have a match," Jax said, moving to Storm's side and tightening the cinch on the saddle. "Do you want to give him a go-round?"

Caden was clearly enthralled, but Seth didn't think the boy was ready to sit in the saddle on his own.

He hesitated, looking first at Jax and then at Rachel, who was still standing by the palomino's side.

"Come on over here, buddy." Jax held out his arms to Caden and the boy immediately responded, barreling into Jax's chest. Caden was really becoming an outgoing child, easily interacting with everyone he met. It had been only a few weeks, but Seth suspected Rachel had a lot to do with his new social skills.

"Seth, you go ahead and mount first," Jax instructed, "and then I'll put this little guy up in front of you."

Seth mounted Storm with no problems. He shifted his weight in the saddle and gathered the reins. He was glad he'd been practicing with the horses at the Bar H ranch so that now he looked more comfortable with Storm than he actually was.

Jax grinned as he propped Caden up in front of Seth and told him to walk the horse around the corral a few times.

"Get up, Storm," Seth said, nudging the horse into a comfortable walk.

"Storm," Caden repeated excitedly, leaning forward to pat the horse's neck. Seth drew the boy back and readjusted his hold around the toddler's waist.

"I think you found your perfect match," Rachel said with a chuckle that Seth joined in on.

"Looks like."

"For a while, this is how you'll want to teach Caden to ride," Jax instructed. "Stay in the saddle with him and let him get used to the horse's movements at different gaits. You'll know when he is ready to try sitting on the saddle on his own. Caden has long legs, but you'll probably want to invest in a children's saddle so you can adjust the stirrups to his height.

"When you make this transition, start by leading him around for a while rather than giving him control of the reins. Before you know it, he'll be a regular little cowboy, galloping across the fields and herding cattle."

"Cowboy! Cowboy!" Caden flapped his feet against the leather, both hands on the saddle horn. "Storm!"

"That settles that, then," Seth said with a laugh. "Storm is our match. How much do I owe you?"

Jax ignored the question for the moment and turned his attention to Rachel and Zooey.

"Monty and Fancy are both saddled and eager to go. Why don't you two mount up and take them for a spin?"

Seth almost laughed out loud at the dismayed expression on Rachel's face, but he had too much sympathy. Riding might be something he already knew how to do, but when it came to other tasks, he'd been thrown in over his head plenty of times in the past month. As for horseback riding, it was harder than it looked, and the sheer size of horses could feel intimidating to a new rider.

Jax tightened the cinch on Monty, and Zooey mounted with surprising ease, waiting with an excited smile as Jax adjusted the stirrups for her. Seth suspected it was not her first time on a horse.

Rachel, on the other hand—

"Um, yeah," she said, clearly flustered. "I don't really do horses."

"No?" Jax adjusted Fancy's cinch and laced his fingers in order to help Rachel mount. "There's a first time for everything, right? Just put your foot right here and I'll boost you into the saddle."

"You have the boots for riding," Seth pointed out,

thoroughly enjoying not being the one completely out of his element for a change.

"Oh, all right." Rachel planted her boot in the cup of Jax's hands and he hoisted her into the saddle.

She sat as straight as a board, clinging to the saddle horn for all she was worth. Jax adjusted the stirrups to fit her height and handed her the reins, but Rachel looked as if she thought the horse was going to bolt off at a dead run.

Seth drew Storm up by her side. She'd encouraged him a lot during the past few weeks. The least he could do was try to repay the kindness.

"Relax. It's sort of like driving a car."

The look she shot him could have started a forest fire.

"Sitting on this horse is *nothing* like driving a car."

"Seriously. You've got to try to relax. Fancy can feel your tension. It will make her nervous."

"Fantastic. Good to know," she said acerbically. "Freaked-out rider on a nervous horse."

"Okay, now for the directions," Jax instructed. "Gently tug the left rein, the horse goes left. Tug right for right. A gentle tug with both reins means stop, and a soft nudge of your heels will get her in gear."

Zooey giggled as she trotted Monty past Rachel and made her way around the corral for the fourth time.

"Come on, Mom. This is fun."

"You have lived in a ranching town for the last fifteen years," Seth said. "I can't believe you've never ridden a horse before."

"You're one to talk. You weren't exactly an expert when you moved back to Serendipity."

"Point taken," he said with a nod. "I rode a little with Luke when we were kids, but I had to relearn a lot when

I returned from the army. Happily, it's like the old cliché about riding a bike. It didn't take me long to remember what I was doing, although I got a little bit saddle sore. The first few days I spent my evenings sitting on ice."

She laughed. "Is that supposed to encourage me?"

He tightened his arm around Caden's waist and urged Storm into a trot.

"Maybe not, but my progress ought to," he called back to her. "I may not have remembered how to ride a horse when I first got back to Serendipity, but, sweetheart, look at me now."

Chapter Seven

Rachel was looking.

It was hard not to—an attractive cowboy teaching his son how to ride a horse. Caden laughing. Seth grinning with the same glow in his blue eyes as when she'd seen him on the auction block performing his beloved parkour for a crowd of people.

And the casual way he'd inserted a term of endearment into the conversation—making it almost a cliché but not quite.

Just enough to throw her for a loop.

It probably meant nothing. Likely, he'd simply misquoted the old saying.

Baby. Sweetheart.

She could see how they could get mixed up.

But his words sent a tremor of awareness down her spine nonetheless.

She closed her eyes, struggling to counteract those thoughts and feelings by reminding herself not to take them seriously. Seth loved to tease. Even if he had meant what he'd said, it was only in good fun, and that was how Rachel was going to take it.

It was the *only* way she would take it.

She ought to be concentrating on staying on Fancy's back, not on analyzing a handsome cowboy's word choice, especially now that Jax had left them for a few minutes to go check on his twin baby girls.

And anyway, that was the shocking thing in this whole situation—she actually *was* staying on the horse. She'd made a few circuits of the corral, and she hadn't slipped off the saddle. This was amazing. Pride welled in Rachel's chest.

She was riding a horse.

Riding a horse!

She couldn't believe where this day had gone. She'd had no intention of riding when she'd come out earlier.

Who knew she would be on a horse, enjoying a relaxed walk around the corral like a regular horsewoman? She was starting to get used to Fancy's slow, rocking rhythm and was adapting to it. She wasn't even clinging to the saddle horn anymore.

She wasn't trotting like Seth and Zooey were, but she counted the fact that she was staying in the saddle at *all* as a win.

"Storm's the one for Caden," Seth said definitively. "Now, what about Fancy and Monty?"

Rachel narrowed her gaze. Caden needed only one horse. But Seth had a sparkle in his eyes that she couldn't quite read.

"What about them?"

"I was just thinking," he said mildly, "that there you are, doing well on Fancy, and Zooey on Monty. You both have good matches, too, right?"

She could see where he was going with this.

Kind of.

He had to be teasing, right? Seth with his typical enthusiastic shortsightedness. A horse was an enormous investment, never mind two. And it wasn't as if she were going to become a regular rider.

Zooey was already beaming in anticipation.

Rachel caught Seth's eye and shook her head. This was *so* not a done deal.

"I have a cat. Myst wouldn't like sharing the house with a couple of horses."

"Mom," Zooey pleaded. "I'll throw in all the allowance I've saved up."

She met Zooey's gaze. "You don't have enough allowance to buy a horse. You used it bidding on Seth, remember?"

"There's plenty of room in the Bar H stable," Seth added. "You two can come out to ride anytime you want, borrowing our saddles and bridles. You don't even need to call first."

There were so many things wrong with this scenario, starting with the fact that she was being ganged up on. She had two sets of puppy-dog eyes on her, pleading for her to give in. That was hardly fair.

"We don't have the money to buy two horses on a whim, never mind paying for the upkeep. Zooey, you can't spend all the money you've saved on a horse."

"But Monty is *my* horse. Can't you see that? I'll do anything. Get a part-time job. Help Seth take care of the horses every evening."

"You have to finish summer school. When are you going to find time for a part-time job? Besides, honey, you're going off to college in two years' time. I'm fairly certain they don't allow horses in dorm rooms."

Zooey's downcast expression nearly shattered Rachel's heart. She hated to have to be the one to douse her daughter's hopes and dreams. She felt worse than when Zooey was eight and she wanted a kitty.

Rachel had lasted two whole days before she'd broken down and they'd visited the local cat rescue to adopt Myst.

She couldn't break down now. This wasn't a cat. It was horses, completely impractical on every level—the biggest being counting on Seth to help shoulder the burden when he wouldn't need her in his life forever.

She might be visiting the Bar H often now, but there would be a time, maybe in the not so far-off future, when Seth would find his foundation as a parent.

He might think he needed her right now, and maybe he did, but eventually he would adjust to life as a single father, and she was sure it wouldn't be long before he found a nice young woman to settle down with—someone without the kind of baggage she carried. Then how would it look for her to show up at the ranch unannounced in order to ride a horse?

Seth looked disappointed, but he nodded, respecting her wishes.

"Just Storm, then. And I'll pick up a children's saddle from Emerson's. I can't wait to teach Caden to ride."

"He's a fast learner," Rachel commented. "I have a feeling he'll be galloping across the fields in no time."

Seth's eyes widened and his Adam's apple bobbed as he swallowed. She could tell he was picturing the scene in his mind, going through every parent's personal crisis of imagining everything that could go wrong.

"In time, of course," she added to quell the flicker of worry in his eyes. "I meant when he is older."

They rode for another half hour before Jax helped

them all dismount and led the horses back to the stable, promising to deliver Storm to the Bar H ranch within the week. Zooey lingered over Monty, feeding him a carrot and stroking his rich dappled mane.

With every turn around the corral, Rachel found it harder and harder not to want to find a way to purchase the horses.

Maybe Jax would take an installment plan. Or she could donate plasma every week for the next year.

She could picture it now, feel it, the lure of true country life, of riding off into the sunset on an amazing animal, perhaps with an equally amazing man.

She might even make it to a trot, eventually.

But her life was too complicated right now to consider adding any kind of change, especially one as large as a horse.

And Zooey had her own set of troubles to worry about. She didn't need any extra distractions.

And as for Rachel, she needed to be concentrating all her time and attention on navigating Zooey through the rough waters of adolescence.

A cat would have to do for now.

And when Zooey moved out and got on with her life, Rachel just might make it a dozen.

She'd be the youngest cat lady ever.

"Earth to Rachel," Seth teased as they drove back to her house. "Man, you were really out there in the ozone somewhere. Care to share? A penny for your thoughts, and all that. Or are we up to a dollar because of inflation?"

What?

He wanted her to tell him that he was looking at a future cat lady?

She didn't think so.

"It's nothing." Because really, it wasn't. "I think I'm just tired from all the excitement of the day."

"You rode a horse."

"I did."

"That's a pretty amazing accomplishment. And trust me. It grows on you."

It certainly seemed to have agreed with Seth. He was getting there, starting to look more at home with his role as rancher. And father.

Really getting there.

But she wouldn't grow to love horseback riding, because she was unlikely to ever do it again.

"You didn't answer my question," he said.

Question?

"Sorry. I must have missed it. What did you say?"

"I asked if you wanted to join me for the town's Fourth of July celebration. Picnic and fireworks. Caden is going to love it. My whole family can't wait to spend quality time with the little guy."

Rachel's heart leaped into her throat and then plunged back down again, lodging in an uncomfortable hard lump in her gut.

Was she hearing right?

Seth was asking her out?

Zooey, who was seated in the backseat of the dual cab next to Caden, stopped tickling and teasing the toddler in order to hear Rachel's response.

Even Caden went still.

The silence was deafening and painful. Seth mostly kept his eyes on the road, but he occasionally glanced in Rachel's direction. She couldn't help but notice the way his fists clenched and unclenched on the steering wheel.

He actually looked nervous.

She thought about simply telling him that she wasn't planning to attend the community event—and then follow through by staying at home.

But she hadn't missed the Fourth of July celebration since the first year she'd moved to Serendipity, when Zooey was just a toddler. And Zooey had been talking about spending time just the two of them for a week now—Rachel didn't want to disappoint her.

Oh, who was she kidding? With the way Zooey had been matchmaking, Rachel knew her daughter would be thrilled to cancel their plans so that Rachel could go out with Seth. But Rachel didn't want to cancel the time with her daughter just so she could pretend for an evening that she had a chance at a romantic relationship that she was certain would never work out. There was no future for her and Seth—and only a small window of time left that she could spend with her daughter before Zooey was off living her own life. She needed to make the most of it.

After that, she'd have the rest of her life to be alone.

"Thank you for the invitation," she said at last.

Seth's grip on the steering wheel immediately relaxed and he grinned.

"Great. Do you want me to pick you up?"

"Let me finish. I appreciate your offer—"

"But?"

"But Zooey and I have special family traditions on the Fourth of July. And besides, you'll be really busy with Caden and your family."

"Mom," Zooey protested, but Rachel held up a hand to stop her from arguing.

"I see." Seth's smile faded and his lips pressed into

a hard, straight line as his jaw tightened and a tick of strain appeared in the corner.

"But again," she repeated, "I do appreciate the offer. It was very kind."

"Mmm." Seth nodded.

The rest of the ride home passed in an uncomfortable, heavy silence. Seth wasn't his usual talkative self and Rachel didn't know what to say. Zooey was curled up, fuming, in the backseat, her earphones in her ears, and Caden had fallen asleep, probably from all of the excitement.

The only thing Rachel could think of to talk about was Caden's new horse, but the conversation had taken a turn so far past that that she thought it would be awkward to return to it.

She was relieved when Seth pulled up in front of her house and she was able to remove herself from the tense situation.

Seth was pleasant enough with his goodbye, so much so that she wondered if she'd imagined the awkwardness between them.

But even if everything was fine between her and Seth, there was another relationship that was on rocky ground. And the outburst started the moment Seth's truck rounded the corner out of sight.

Zooey turned on her, her face red with fury.

"Mom. How could you?"

"How could I what?"

"Seth asked you out—and you turned him down."

"Yes, I did."

"But why? Seth is a great guy. I could tell he was really upset when you said you wouldn't go with him."

"I know."

"Then why? I know you like him."

"I think we've already established that he is a nice man."

"No, Mom. I mean, you *like* him, like him. You should call him or text him or something and let him know you made a mistake and you want to go out with him."

"I don't *like* like anyone. I'm not in high school anymore," Rachel snapped, and then instantly regretted it. "I'm sorry, Zooey. I didn't mean to be short with you or minimize your opinion. It's just— Well, it's a lot more complicated than that now that I'm an adult. I can't just consider how I do or do not feel about him."

"Why is it when adults don't want to face something, they say *it's complicated*? Everything in life is complicated. What advice would you give me if I was the one in your circumstances?"

Rachel sighed. "To follow your heart and not let anything get in the way of your dreams."

"Exactly. So look in the mirror when you say that and ask yourself, why aren't you?"

"Because you still have two years of school left." Rachel grasped at the first excuse that entered her head.

Zooey's eyes went big. "What does dating Seth have to do with me?"

"Everything. You're the most important person in my life. I want to make sure I'm always there for you, to help you navigate through the rough waters that are ahead of you—if and when you need my help, I mean. That's where my attention should be—not on some man I barely know. Besides, I'm busy with the day care."

"But not too busy to help Seth with Caden."

"That's different."

"*How* is that different? You're spending all of your spare time with Seth anyway. Why not make one of those times an official date?"

Because...because...

She was scared to death.

"You're right. I enjoy helping Seth with Caden, and I love how much you and Caden have bonded. But what if I date Seth and we end up breaking up? It won't just be my heart that is broken. Our relationship would affect you and Caden, as well. Can you imagine the awkwardness we'd all feel when Seth brought Caden to day care?"

Rachel was speaking the truth from experience. In the past, the few times she'd been in a relationship she felt was serious enough to bring Zooey into the picture, it had always resulted in disasters. It took a lot for her to trust a man enough to even introduce him to her daughter.

And when it didn't work out?

She couldn't just hide out and nurse her broken heart—it would upset Zooey if she saw that Rachel was depressed. So she had to be cheerful and upbeat while explaining why her ex-boyfriend would no longer be coming around. There were no easy answers.

"So you've already brought yourself all the way from the beginning of a relationship to a breakup in one fell swoop, when you haven't even gone out with him once. Nice, Mom."

"I'm just being practical."

"No. You're not. You're concealing yourself behind excuses so you won't have to deal with the possibility of failure. You can't live your life that way. Don't hide behind me, Mom, or make me a justification for why you aren't living your own life, chasing your own dreams. That's not fair to me or to you. Two years is going to pass in a heartbeat. Even right now, I've got my own life to live. School to attend. Friends to hang out with. I love you, Mom, but it's time for you to go start living for *you*. I want the best for you, just like you always have for me. And trust me on this—Seth is the best."

They hugged for a long time and then Zooey kissed Rachel's cheek before racing inside and upstairs to her room.

Rachel stood in the middle of the front lawn for a long time. She felt as if someone had replaced the blood that ran through her veins with lead.

She'd raised an amazing young lady.

Was it true, what Zooey was saying?

That she was making excuses, hiding behind her daughter so she didn't have to expose her heart and risk being hurt?

She might be protecting herself from pain by putting up walls around her heart, but she was also keeping other emotions out—and keeping other people at arm's length. Special people who could potentially change her life for the better.

Maybe she should call Seth and tell him she'd made a mistake. Maybe she should give the two of them a chance.

She pulled out her cell phone, stared at it a moment and then promptly replaced it in the back pocket of her jeans.

She felt her chest squeeze the breath out of her lungs just thinking about trying to move forward with her life.

Did she really dare open her heart again?

* * *

The Fourth of July dawned bright and clear without a cloud in the sky. A wonderful day for a picnic and an ideal sky for the spectacular grand fireworks finale.

For Seth, though, this morning wasn't sunshine and roses. His mood was closer to cloudy with a chance of rain and nothing he did helped snap him out of it.

At first Seth hadn't understood why Rachel turned him down. After all the time they'd been spending together recently, he'd thought Rachel and Zooey would enjoy spending the Fourth of July celebration with him and Caden, and with his family—the Howells and the Davenports.

He had to admit he was disappointed. And his ego had taken a direct hit.

He was eager for his sister, Samantha, and brother-in-law, Will, as well as his parents to get better acquainted with Rachel, the woman who'd helped him so much in his transition from bachelor to single dad.

He'd analyzed the conversation over and over again in his mind before he finally realized the truth of what had happened.

Rachel had thought he was asking her out on a date. And that was why she'd said no.

Wow.

Ouch.

And here he thought his ego had taken a hit when he believed she was turning down a family get-together.

If he was right in his conclusion, Rachel had turned *him* down.

Personally.

She was willing to help him when it came to Caden,

but that was as far as it went. She didn't want to spend time with him socially.

And the worst part was, now that the notion of asking Rachel out on a date had entered his thick head, it wouldn't leave him alone.

He *should* have asked her out on a date for the town festivities.

Of course, she would have turned him down anyway. But he should have asked, with those intentions in mind.

Yes, they both had their fair share of responsibilities that would make pursuing a relationship challenging—and risky. It made his gut tighten just thinking about the possibility of failure. But when had he ever given up just because something was hard to do?

He wouldn't have succeeded as a soldier if he'd quit when the going got tough.

He was attracted to Rachel. He couldn't help but admire her giving, caring, empathetic heart. When she committed herself to something or someone, she went all in. The way she'd stepped in to help him with Caden was the perfect example of that.

He and Rachel got along well. They'd become good friends. And Caden and Zooey had bonded in a special way.

So what was it about him that had caused her to balk?

They had physical chemistry. At times, when their eyes met, electricity crackled between them.

It couldn't be one-sided. He knew she felt it, too.

So, why, then?

He still hadn't come up with a satisfactory answer when he met with his family on the community green later that afternoon.

Even with his thoughts heavily on Rachel, he was

looking forward to attending the first Fourth of July picnic with his family since he'd returned to Serendipity. The last time he'd had the pleasure, he'd been a senior in high school.

Man, how things had changed since then.

Seth wasn't the same man he'd been when he left town. The army had forced him to start the process of growing up, but it was accepting the guardianship of Caden, and the weeks that had followed as he learned how to be a father, that had really made him a man. With his newfound maturity, he could look at a celebration like this and really appreciate all that went into it—and what it meant to be part of such a terrific community. He could hardly believe that just a month ago, he'd been intent on leaving this all behind.

Serendipity was where he belonged. Especially on a day like today, when there was so much to enjoy.

He was particularly looking forward to partaking of his mother's homemade country cooking. Amanda Howell was known far and wide for the bounty she served up at their bed-and-breakfast. He wasn't much of a cook. Straight meat and vegetables, usually grilled.

Sometimes even a fitness nut needed to cheat.

Even more than the food, though, he was highly anticipating the opportunity to spend quality time with his parents and his older sister, Samantha. Sam had married Will Davenport, who had served in the same army unit as Seth and was now not only his brother in arms but his brother-in-law.

And then there were his nieces and nephew—seven-year-old Genevieve and two-year-old twins Charlie and Melody. Even with the slower pace small-town living offered, everyone had busy schedules, and it was precious time when the whole family could be together.

His mom and dad owned and ran the town's only bed-and-breakfast, while Sam and Will took care of Sam's Grocery, which had been passed down through the family for several generations.

Upon arriving at the already-crowded community green, his mother immediately relieved him of Caden, while Sam and Will's twins tackled Seth, anxious to wrestle their "fun uncle" to the ground.

He kept his eye out for Rachel and Zooey but didn't see them in the crowd. He wasn't sure what he was going to do or say when and if he *did* see them.

Approach them and give his invitation a second try?

Honor Rachel's wishes and leave her to enjoy her family day with Zooey?

While the adults set up the food, he entertained all of the children with parkour tricks, teaching the younger ones front somersaults in the grass and crab-walking.

Before he knew it, he had a much larger audience and over a dozen young participants. Everyone, it seemed, wanted to get in on the action. Several of the teenagers were trying different moves—handstands, banking off tree trunks or hanging off branches.

"It looks like you're a hit."

Seth's heart skipped at the sound of Rachel's voice. He hadn't seen her and her daughter approach. Zooey's attention had already been diverted by nearby friends, and she was showing them how to do a banking backflip off a bench. She'd been practicing.

"All in good fun."

"Better than good. You have a gift. Look how the children and teenagers respond to you. You've even got a few teenagers as part of this group who are here from Redemption Ranch." It took him a moment to make the connection, but then he remembered the ministry program he'd heard about from his family in their letters and phone calls while he was overseas. Alexis, a local rancher, brought out teens who'd committed minor criminal offenses and let them work off their court-mandated community service hours on her ranch, where she tried to help them turn their lives around with love, prayer and a good dose of hard work.

Seth hadn't visited the ranch himself, but he figured if there was anyone on earth who could push a bunch of surly teenagers into being better people by sheer force of will, Alexis—one of his sister's best friends and possibly the most determined woman in the world—could do it.

"Alexis will be thrilled to see how excited they are," Rachel continued. "Those kids come from bad situations and need a little tough love. Parkour might be good therapy for them. You ought to think about offering them some classes."

"Exercise is always good therapy, especially for kids."

"True, although some of us don't find quite the joy in it that you do. I like to dance as much as the next woman, but there are still many days when I have to force myself out of bed early so I can stick in my dancing workout DVD before my itty-bitties start showing up for day care."

"I have days like that, too," he admitted, helping Caden somersault forward and backward on the soft grass.

"No way. You're going to college to major in athletic

training. Working out is probably the highlight of your day."

"Okay, I'll admit it doesn't happen often. I love being outdoors and stretching my muscles while I take in the fresh air. But I don't think college is in the works for me, at least not right now. I've got the ranch and Caden. That's more than enough to keep me busy."

Rachel dropped onto the lawn next to Caden and he immediately crawled into her lap. Seth sat cross-legged next to her, and within a minute he had Charlie and Melody, one on each knee.

"I wasn't sure I was going to see you today," he confessed, deciding not to beat around the bush. Rachel was a straight shooter and didn't care to play games, unless they were the fun kind and involved children.

She looked him right in the eye and nodded. "To be honest, I wasn't, either."

"What changed your mind?"

"In part, at least, a conversation I had with Zooey. She made me see I was hiding behind her, using her as an excuse for not living my own life."

Seth's heart welled. "She's a smart young lady."

"Yes, she is. And she's right. I don't want to get to the end of my life and realize I missed out because I was afraid to put myself out there." She shrugged and flashed him a rueful grin. "I don't want to end up a cat lady."

He tried to chuckle and choked instead, then swallowed around the lump that formed in his throat. She still thought he'd asked her out on a date, and yet here she was.

Maybe he ought to leave well enough alone and make

the most of this evening, but somehow that didn't feel right.

For one thing, he really did want his family to have the opportunity to spend time with Rachel and see what he saw in her. And then there was Zooey. He wanted her to join in the family gathering, as well.

"The other day, when I asked you to the picnic—"

He paused, trying to choose his words carefully so he didn't screw this up.

"And like an idiot, I turned you down," she said before he could finish.

He grinned. "You're not an idiot. You were protecting yourself, which I respect. That's always a smart thing to do." He cleared his throat. "That said, in full disclosure, I wasn't actually asking you out on a date."

Her gaze widened to epic proportions and she practically gaped at him. He'd definitely caught her off guard with that statement.

"You weren't?"

"What I *was* trying to do—badly, apparently—was to suggest our families celebrate together. My parents have a very high opinion of you, and I thought you might enjoy spending time with my family. I know they'd like to spend time with you. Then again," he said, lifting up his arms so the twins could crawl over him like a jungle gym, "maybe you'd rather have a quiet celebration with your daughter."

"As you can see," she said, gesturing toward Zooey, who was still trying parkour moves with her friends, "my daughter has her own idea of what a fun Fourth of July celebration looks like."

"So you'll stay?"

"Yes. But—I want to be clear about this—it was never a date?"

"Well, no, but— That is, I—" he stammered.

How in the world was he going to explain that while his first thought had been for a family gathering, he now thought the idea of a date between them was spot-on?

Maybe he should have left well enough alone.

"Yes?"

He shook his head. "No. Never mind. I'm glad you and Zooey showed up."

Who was the idiot now?

"Shall I add the food I brought to your family's goodies? I don't cook as well as your mother."

"I'm sure your dishes are just fine. My motto is, the more food, the merrier." He patted his stomach and licked his lips to accentuate his point.

Rachel handed Caden off to Zooey and went to lay her offerings down with the Howells' already-tasty smorgasbord.

Meanwhile, Seth was furiously considering how to get some time alone with Rachel. He didn't know how it was going to happen, or when, but he was determined he'd create some kind of dating atmosphere at some point tonight, and he'd be watching for his moment.

"Soup's on," Rachel called in an animated tone, and everyone gathered to eat and share fellowship.

The picnic dinner was the most enjoyable he'd ever had, surrounded by family and friends and with Rachel by his side and Caden in his lap.

He thought he might get a little ribbing for having invited Rachel to celebrate with them. He was the baby of the family and they liked to give him a hard time.

He was taken aback, however, by how warmly they

welcomed Rachel to their meal, as if she'd belonged there all of her life, as if she were already part of the family and not an invited guest.

Even Zooey fit in, dividing her time between conversing with the adults over what her plans were after high school and playing with the children. She had Rachel's nurturing gift with the kids, taking seven-year-old Genevieve under her wing and making her feel special by engaging her in girl talk and getting into a serious, animated discussion about her favorite books.

It wasn't long after everyone had cleaned their plates and what was left of the food had been put away that Seth noticed a couple of teenagers he didn't recognize had joined Zooey.

Rachel, who'd been deep in conversation with Samantha, had noticed, too, and quickly excused herself to head in Zooey's direction.

Seth, who was playing with Caden, followed her.

"Hi, Abigail," Rachel said to a tall, thin auburn-haired girl. "My, it's been a long time since I've seen you. I remember when you were just a little tyke. Now you've grown up into a pretty young woman."

The girl blushed, her pinkened cheeks clashing with the color of her hair.

Rachel's gaze shifted to the teenage boy standing with them. He was a clean-cut kid, dressed in khaki Bermuda shorts and a bright green polo shirt, with well-trimmed blond hair combed back off his forehead.

Before Rachel could say a word, the young man reached out to shake her hand.

"Hello, Ms. Perez. My name is Dawson McAllister, ma'am. My mom and I just moved into town."

"Glad to meet you, Dawson."

Rachel had told Seth about the questionable friends Zooey had made during summer school, teenagers she'd been afraid might influence Zooey into dangerous behavior.

Seth briefly wondered if these might be the kids she'd meant, but he immediately decided that wasn't the case.

These two were far too polite to be trouble, and he could see from Rachel's relaxed smile that she was genuinely happy to see the girl and meet the boy. Both teenagers were wholesome looking and respectful to the adults.

"His mom is a single parent like you and Seth," Zooey added excitedly. "But she has the flu and can't make it to the fireworks tonight."

"I'm sorry to hear that," said Seth. "You'll have to introduce us later."

"Mom, is it okay if we hang out for a while?" Zooey asked. "I promise we'll stay on the green."

"Just be sure to find us right after the fireworks display is finished," Rachel said.

As soon as the teenagers were out of hearing distance, Rachel turned to Seth with an amused smile. "I overheard a conversation between Zooey and Abigail the other day on the phone. Dawson is the new guy in town, and I think Zooey might be crushing on him."

Seth laughed. "I'm no judge of looks, but I like his character. They both look pretty respectable to me."

"They are good kids. I'm so thankful to God that she's found better friends."

Seth was getting used to Rachel attributing all of the circumstances in her life to God's care.

When there was good, like Zooey's new friends, she

praised God. When she bumped up against trials and tribulations—and she'd had many—she had faith that the Lord would see her through.

Had God brought Rachel into his life?

The thought stunned him, shifting his view entirely.

Rachel had always been there, in the exact right times and places, precisely when he needed her. There were too many factors involved for it to be a mere coincidence that she'd come into his life when she had.

For the first time in a very long time he saw God's hand at work in his life. The Lord wasn't far off somewhere in the high heavens, too busy to care for His creations.

He was here. Now. Watching over His people and blessing them.

Seth had only to look around him to realize the number of blessings he had to be thankful for—his family, his friends, and most of all, Rachel and Caden, and even Zooey.

"Who is that?" Rachel asked, nodding toward a thin woman with platinum-blond hair crossing the green. "I don't recognize her. Maybe she's Dawson's mom and she decided to come out for the fireworks."

Seth shrugged. Whoever she was, she stuck out like a sore thumb, wobbling along in four-inch spiked heels and wearing a skirt cut well above her knees. He knew zilch about purses, but he suspected the giant one she carried in the crook of her elbow cost more than he made in the army in a month. Her short, stylish hair and heavily applied makeup completed the odd picture.

It wasn't that she looked unattractive; her outfit just seemed overdone and out of place in this relaxed community gathering. This woman was definitely not from the country.

He watched as she stopped and spoke to Jo and Frank Spencer. They exchanged an animated dialogue—Jo was always animated, but this time it seemed to Seth that she was especially vivacious.

But then Jo pointed directly at him and waved.

His skin prickled and the hair stood up on the back of his neck as he apprehensively returned her wave.

He didn't know why his pulse ratcheted up and his lungs suddenly felt as if he were breathing lead.

It was probably Dawson's mom, he reminded himself as the woman started toward him. Who else could it be?

"Seth?" Rachel threaded her hand in the crook of his arm. Her gaze was also on the woman crossing the green, and her tone was wary. He sensed she was experiencing the same disquiet he was.

"Seth Howell?" The woman's ice-blue eyes bore right through him, making his insides feel frosty.

"Who's asking?"

Rachel squeezed his arm.

Maybe he did sound a little short with her. He tried to smile.

The woman didn't answer him. Instead, she glanced around their picnic area, and suddenly her face broke out into what Seth thought was the fakest smile he'd ever seen.

She made a beeline for Charlie but stopped short before him, leaning down and barely patting him on the head, as if she was afraid he might get dirt on her fancy outfit.

No chance of that—Charlie hunched back and looked for his father, instinctively not trusting the woman.

When he made a sudden movement and she snatched her hand back in alarm, he rushed into Will's outstretched arms.

The stranger definitely had everyone's attention in their little group now.

"How cute my little nephew is," she crowed, awkwardly dropping her hand to her side.

"Nephew?" Will repeated, his brow lowering.

"Ma'am, I think you must be mistaking us for someone else. How can we help you?" Seth asked, trying to remain polite and ignoring the fact that it seemed she'd asked Jo specifically for him and the question of what that might mean.

"No, no. That redheaded old lady over there said this is where I'd find him."

"Find your nephew?" Rachel clarified.

The blonde nodded.

"I'm afraid you're mistaken. This is Charlie, Samantha and Will Davenport's son."

"Oh, I—" she stammered, looking confused for a moment. "No, no. Not Charlie."

She looked around and Seth's heart stopped beating when her gaze landed on Caden, who was playing with Genevieve and was unaware of what was going on around him.

"Why, there he is," she said, as if she hadn't first accosted Charlie with the same intentions.

Her false smile returned in spades and it was all Seth could do not to race forward and snatch his son away before she could get to him.

He moved closer but at a slower pace, ready at a moment's notice to go with his original plan.

"It's my little nephew. *Caden.*"

Chapter Eight

Rachel's heart plummeted at the words. This woman could be none other than Tracy's sister, Trish.

What was she doing in Serendipity?

Seth had said she hadn't had anything to do with Luke and Tracy in the past. She'd completely alienated herself from her sister. She hadn't even shown up for Tracy's funeral and had sent a lawyer in her stead for the reading of Luke and Tracy's will.

If she remembered correctly, Seth had said Trish had never seen Caden in person, not even as an infant. She certainly didn't have a clue who he was now. She'd scared poor Charlie half to death with her inept approach.

"Trish?" Seth asked, clearly having come to the same conclusion. "Trish Ward?"

When the woman's gaze shifted from Caden to Seth, Rachel used the opportunity to steal Caden into her arms, which she hoped would offer the boy a sense of security in what was looking to be a confusing mess.

Caden was an intelligent, sensitive child and she knew he would perceive the undercurrent of tension that was already crackling between Trish and the Howells, who had gathered around Seth, presenting a united—and slightly intimidating—front before the woman.

"That's right. I'm Trish. Caden's auntie. And I've traveled a long way to see the child, so I would appreciate your cooperation in the matter."

She sounded as if she were brokering some kind of business deal, not asking to visit her nephew.

For a moment, Seth's expression appeared torn, but then he straightened his shoulders decisively and reached to take Caden from Rachel's arms.

She closed ranks, standing side by side with Seth, her hand on his shoulder to let him know she was there for him and offer him silent reassurance and support.

"This is Caden," he said cautiously.

Trish studied Caden for a second but made no move to reach out and take him.

Which was good for her, because Rachel was fighting against a profound protective urge to step between Trish and Caden and hold her arms out to imitate a physical wall.

She wasn't sure what it was about Trish that set off all of Rachel's internal alarms, but she knew she wasn't the only one feeling it. Every adult in the vicinity, including Seth, had the same expression on their faces.

Perhaps it was that Trish looked so out of place among the country people. Maybe it was that she was so awkward with children. Then there was the fact that she hadn't made the least effort to see Caden in the past when Tracy was alive.

She hadn't even gone to her own sister's funeral.

And now she was standing in the middle of Serendipity's community green during a traditional celebration, dressed in outlandishly inappropriate clothing and asking after Caden because—

Why *was* she here?

"I've traveled a long way to get here," Trish said, sounding annoyed. "A ridiculously long plane ride, not to mention the time it took to get to this podunk town in the middle of Nowhere, Texas. My limo driver said it wasn't even on the map."

"You should have rented a car," Amanda Howell suggested, with only the tiniest trace of sarcasm in her tone. "It would have been much cheaper."

Trish sniffed. "I won't be staying long."

Well, that was a relief, anyway. Perhaps she'd just had a touch of conscience and thought she ought to check in on her nephew. Now that the woman had seen that Caden was happy and healthy, well cared for and loved by everyone, maybe she would leave it at that.

And just plain *leave*.

"Why *are* you here?" Seth asked, pulling Caden even tighter against his chest.

"I have a perfect right to see my nephew."

"True," Seth agreed, his tone flat. "I'm not questioning that. I guess what I am wondering is why you're here *now*. Let's be honest, Trish. You haven't shown much interest in Caden in the past, so I have to ask myself what changed that brought you here?"

Rachel bristled. Trish hadn't shown *any* interest in Caden in the past. And now all of a sudden she was so concerned about her nephew?

Rachel didn't think so.

The real question was—what was in it for her?

Then again, maybe she wasn't being fair to Trish.

Rachel was in no position to judge anyone. Technically, she wasn't involved in this situation at all.

Except she was.

She had somehow become personally invested in Seth and Caden. She cared what happened to them.

She cared about *them*.

And though Trish hadn't said as much, Rachel suspected she was a threat to them in some way. It only remained for her to figure out how.

And in the meantime, to try to show patience. And grace. The Lord could have worked on Trish's conscience. No one was beyond His help. Granted, she didn't know how to act around children, but that didn't mean she was here out of anything but the best intentions and not the selfishness Rachel had automatically attributed to her.

Rachel decided to take a wait-and-see attitude.

Trish shrugged and flashed a not-quite-sincere smile. "Well, of course I want to see how my nephew is getting on, especially now that Tracy's gone and Caden has a new—"

Trish paused and gave Seth an appreciative once-over that sent a chill down Rachel's spine.

"—guardian," Trish finished, her alto voice thick and humming with pleasure.

Apparently, the woman was much more adept at interacting with adult males than she was with toddlers. What she probably didn't know was that not every single man walking the planet was susceptible to her charms.

Rachel felt Seth's muscles stiffen and his jaw ticked with strain. She could tell that he didn't enjoy Trish's flirtatious manner with him any more than Charlie had cared for her disingenuous pat on the head.

"As you can see, I've got my whole family here celebrating the Fourth of July. Would you like to join us? We've got plenty of food left over," Seth said, with far more grace than Rachel imagined she could have mustered.

Trish's cool blue gaze flicked over the family and she pursed her lips.

"No, I don't think so," she said abruptly. "I have the limo driver waiting for me. If you will direct me to the nearest hotel—preferably five stars—I will get out of your way so you can have your family time. Seth, you and I will meet to discuss Caden later—in *private*."

Rachel seethed at the way Trish ordered Seth around. Despite her resolve to keep an open mind, that clinched Rachel's opinion of her. Trish didn't really want to interact with Caden or see how he was faring, and she most definitely didn't want to have anything to do with Caden's new extended family.

Trish wouldn't mind spending time with *Seth*, maybe, but Rachel was equally as sure he didn't want to have a thing to do with Trish.

"I'm sorry to say we don't have a hotel here in Serendipity," Samantha said, not sounding particularly sorry at all. "If that's what you need, you'll have to ask your limo driver to take you into one of the larger cities. Amarillo has some nice hotels."

"Or you could stay with us," Samuel offered. "We're no five-star resort, but we run a nice little bed-and-breakfast down by the stream. You'll have your own private cabin with heat and indoor plumbing, and my

Amanda here is well-known for her homemade country cooking."

He paused and tossed Amanda an affectionate grin before returning his gaze to Trish. "You'll be quite comfortable. We even have Wi-Fi in the main lodge."

Trish looked aghast, as if the thought of spending the night in a country cabin was akin to camping out in a tent in the middle of a rugged mountain terrain.

With bears.

And coyotes.

With or without Wi-Fi.

"I think not," Trish said, not even bothering to thank Samuel for the offer.

Rachel didn't think she'd ever met anyone quite as rude and arrogant as Trish Ward.

"That is a very sweet offer, Samuel," Rachel said, feeling like she needed to cover for Trish's glaring lapse in good manners.

Trish appeared to take the hint.

"Yes, yes. Of course. Thank you, Samuel, but I think I'd prefer to find a hotel. Amarillo, did you say?"

Samantha nodded, a satisfied smile creeping up her lips.

When Trish wasn't looking, Samantha caught Rachel's eyes and mouthed, *Or Mars*.

It was all Rachel could do to withhold her laughter. This was the wrong time and place for that.

Trish fished around in her enormous designer purse for a moment before withdrawing her cell phone.

"Punch in your number for me, will you, Seth?" Her smile became so syrupy sweet it turned Rachel's stomach.

Seth's jaw was still set and pulsing as he put in his number.

"I'll call you later so we can get together when you're not so...*busy* with other people."

"You do that," Seth said, although it was evident from his tone that he hoped she would not.

Rachel hoped she would not, although she knew better than to hope they'd seen the last of Trish. For whatever reason—and it very obviously wasn't to visit Caden—Trish Ward had traveled clear across the country to Serendipity.

And she wasn't going away.

Seth thought he might be sick as he watched Trish Ward with her ridiculous platinum hair wobble her way off the community green. Several people tried to engage her in conversation, but she just lifted her chin and ignored them.

Not even a polite nod toward the friendly folks who were just trying to welcome a stranger in their midst.

He didn't know how people acted where she came from, but in his part of the country, her behavior was considered just plain rude.

And wasn't it wonderful that she was Caden's aunt—by blood. He didn't even want to think about the possible implications of that fact.

He pulled Caden tight to him and breathed in his little-boy scent—something that two months ago he never would have imagined as being so sweet and comforting. Caden had become completely vital to his existence.

The toddler wasn't merely a responsibility in his life anymore, or a sacrifice he had to make for the sake of his deceased friends.

Caden was his baby blessing.

The toddler objected to being held so closely and squirmed and wiggled until Seth set him down. Seth let him go.

The boy was safe for now, anyway.

There were still times when Seth woke up late at night in a cold sweat, wondering why God had allowed the sniper to take Luke and not him. But he'd finally come to accept that, for whatever reason, he and Caden now had an inseparable bond together—one that went beyond blood and straight to Seth's heart.

But Trish?

She *was* related to Caden by blood. Seth had Luke and Tracy's will naming him Caden's legal guardian, but what if Trish was here to make trouble and try to claim custody for herself?

"Hey." Rachel's voice was gentle as she laid a hand on his arm. "Are you okay?"

Seth took a deep, cleansing breath and slowly let it out, then picked off his hat and raked his fingers through his hair. He was getting a killer headache.

"Honestly? I don't know." He shook his head. "To tell the truth, I'm not sure of anything anymore."

"Don't second-guess yourself. Luke and Tracy knew what they were doing when they wrote their will and asked you to be Caden's guardian. I'm sure they made sure that it's completely ironclad. That's what they wanted for Caden—*you*. Whatever Trish wants or thinks she's entitled to, don't forget that *you* are Caden's daddy now, and nothing Trish does or says can change that."

His heart warmed. It meant a lot that he had Rachel's trust and support. He wished he had the words to express how grateful he was to have her near him, but his throat closed and he got all tongue-tied.

Samantha approached, holding Caden's hand as he toddled around on the grass.

"You look like you're about to jump out of your skin, little brother."

He replaced his hat and stood to his full height, towering over Samantha.

"I haven't been your *little* brother in years."

Samantha jerked the brim of his hat down so it covered his eyes. "Maybe, but I'm still smarter than you are."

"You wish."

He might not have lost his sense of humor, but stress was still rolling off him in waves, and he knew Samantha was just trying to cheer him up.

"No, seriously, I came to tell you that Mom and I want to spend some quality time with Caden," Samantha said. "I don't think there's any concern about Trish returning this evening. Why don't you and Rachel take a walk around the green—to clear your big head."

"You two are terrible." Rachel chuckled at the back-and-forth interchange between the siblings.

Samantha snorted. "You should have seen us when we were little tykes."

"Yeah," Seth agreed. "She could outwrestle me until I hit my adolescent growth spurt."

"You'd better believe it," Samantha crowed.

"She'd start it, and then when Mom and Dad would come in, she'd blame it on me and I'd be the one who got in trouble. Dad said I wasn't supposed to wrestle girls, but Samantha isn't a girl. She's my sister."

Samantha snickered.

"And worse, she still pinches me when she doesn't get her way."

Samantha demonstrated, pinching Seth's cheeks like she would a toddler's. "Isn't he just the cutest little thing you've ever seen?"

"Cut it out." Heat filled his cheeks, and not because his sister had been pinching them. He wasn't sure he wanted to know Rachel's answer to that question. What if it was another ego-deflating reply? He swatted Samantha's hand away.

Rachel's chuckle turned into outright laughter. "I never had a brother or sister to spar with, and Zooey is an only child. Seeing you two together makes me wish she could have had a sibling."

"Zooey's really good with children," Samantha observed. "I saw her playing with Caden earlier and he just adores her."

"Like mother, like daughter," Seth agreed, feeling oddly proud about the statement.

"Speaking of Zooey—where is she?" Samantha asked. "I can keep an eye on her, too, if you want."

"Off with her friends," Rachel answered. "I told her to be back right after the fireworks display is finished."

"Great. Then there is no reason for you two not to take that walk I mentioned."

Samantha winked and mouthed the words *Be good* to him. The heat in his face turned to a burning open flame. Thankfully, she hadn't voiced her comment aloud, and Rachel didn't appear to have noticed.

Otherwise, he would have had to string his sister up by her ears.

He still might.

He mock-scowled at her and took Rachel's hand.

"Come on. Let's get out of here before Samantha finds something else to embarrass me about."

He didn't realize that he was practically running off the green until Rachel pulled him up, her breath coming in short gasps.

"Look, I know you want to put some distance between yourself and your mischievous sister, but if you don't slow your pace, you're going to be dragging deadweight here in a second. I'm about to pass out. You may be a marathon runner, but me, not so much."

He laughed. "Sorry. Do you want to sit for a moment?" He gestured to a nearby bench.

"Just for a minute, if you don't mind. It won't take me long to catch my breath."

He led her to the bench and sat down beside her, never once letting go of her hand.

She didn't seem to mind—and he needed the human contact right now just to ground him after that confrontation with Trish.

Rachel stared at their clasped hands, and for a moment he thought she might pull away, but instead she threaded her fingers through his and gave his hand a light squeeze.

"I'm sorry Trish had to show up and ruin your family get-together," she said softly. Regretfully.

"Yeah. What is *with* that?"

"I don't know. She's a strange cookie. I just don't understand why she's suddenly shown up in Serendipity, pretending to be interested in Caden."

"You got that, too, that she's just pretending to be interested in Caden, huh?"

"It was kind of hard to miss. I think she frightened poor Charlie half to death. As someone who works with children on a regular basis, I can tell you definitively that that woman has never been around a child in her life."

"Which makes me wonder..."

"Why she's here now," Rachel finished for him. "Because it can't be for Caden's sake."

"Exactly." He put his other hand over their threaded fingers and gently stroked the inside of her wrist with his thumb.

They were both silent for a moment before he shared what was on his mind.

"Do you think—" He inhaled deeply and plunged on. "Is it possible she's just here to meet her nephew? That she suddenly realized she was making a mistake to alienate her family, and she wants to make amends now?"

"It's possible," Rachel said, quietly and deliberately. "But not probable. Nothing I saw or heard today made me think she was really here because she cares for Caden in any way—except that I had the oddest feeling she wanted something from him."

He cringed, and Rachel tightened her grip on his hand.

"I agree. I want to think the best of her. She's Tracy's sister. And even though they were estranged, I know Tracy loved her and always wanted to reconcile. But something about Trish rubs me the wrong way. She doesn't seem...sincere."

"Which leads us back to square one," Rachel said with a sigh. "Why is the woman here, and what does she want with Caden?"

"Nothing good, I don't imagine. Honestly, I'm afraid even to speculate."

"I understand how you feel. The magnitude of possibilities are frightening, to say the least. But I think if we talk through it, you'll be better prepared when you meet with her."

"My gut turns over every time I think about having to see her again. I don't want to hear anything she has to say, and I don't know why she's so adamant about meeting with me alone."

"Don't you?"

Rachel could have been teasing him, but Seth doubted it. Her tone was dead serious, and he knew she was thinking the same thing he was—that Tracy was after him romantically.

"Well, if that's what she's looking for, she's barking up the wrong tree."

"I think finding out that Caden's guardian is a handsome single man is just frosting on the cake for her."

"I'm no one's frosting." Despite the seriousness of their conversation, one side of his mouth kicked up.

Rachel had just said she thought he was handsome.

Well, she'd said she imagined *Trish* thought he was handsome, but wasn't that the same thing?

Too bad thinking about the coming meeting with Trish had to spoil the moment for him. He wasn't able to revel in Rachel's attention.

"What I don't get is why she was asking about Caden when she clearly had no interest in spending time with him. I'll tell you this—I'm not inclined to let her anywhere near my child."

"I think she wants something from him."

"What could Caden possibly give her? He's only two, for crying out loud."

She shook her head. "I don't know. Maybe there was something in the will."

"She wasn't at the reading of the will—she sent a lawyer in her stead."

"Did they leave Trish anything that might somehow be misconstrued to be connected with Caden?"

Seth furrowed his brow. "I don't think so. I have to admit I don't really remember the details. I was pretty broken up having Tracy die so soon after Luke. And I was trying to wrap my mind around the reality that I'd just become the legal guardian of their son. Everything from that time is really foggy. I assume Trish was left something. I think the lawyers met together afterward. If there were any concerns, wouldn't the lawyers have brought it up then? I never heard that she was contesting the will or anything."

As soon as the words were out of his mouth, the air left his lungs in a whoosh, as if he'd been sucker punched.

"Could she really do that, do you think?" he asked, his voice ragged.

"Contest the will? I don't know. Maybe. But why would she *want* to do that? There's no doubt in my mind that she has no interest in raising Caden herself."

"I don't know." He inhaled sharply and then shoved out a breath. "I just don't know."

"I don't, either, but if that's what she has in mind, we'll contest it."

She caught what she'd said, and even in the dark of twilight, Seth could see the blush that slashed across her cheeks. He didn't know what she had to be embarrassed about. He was glad she was by his side, supporting him.

"I mean *you* will contest any claim that she makes to

challenge the will. It seems to me that it's all straightforward, right? In black and white. And you know Luke and Tracy would have made it airtight."

"Well, if it comes to that, and I pray it doesn't, I'll make an appointment with the lawyer who executed Luke and Tracy's will. But frankly, I have to say I'm concerned. Trish seems a little off-kilter to me. I don't know how to deal with that. Plus, she came in a limo and insisted on staying in a five-star hotel. I'm guessing she has way more money than me—enough to hire a fancy lawyer. What if they find a way around my guardianship?"

Rachel grimaced. "Okay, it was my idea to speculate, and now I'm going to say we ought to stop. I'm sorry, Seth. All I've managed to do here is stress you out even more than you already were, and that was the last thing I wanted to do. We don't know anything yet. Let's wait and see how it plays out. I'm certain Samantha wanted me to help you calm down when she suggested we take a walk together."

Seth choked on his breath and it was his turn to blush. "What do you mean?"

Maybe she had seen Samantha's wink and the teasingly mouthed words after all. But Rachel only looked confused by his question.

"She knows we've become close friends. I figure she thought I could be a sounding board for you to work through your worries and settle a little bit—not rile you up as I've apparently done."

"Close friends," he repeated, unlacing his fingers from hers and putting his arm across the back of the bench so he could turn her way and hopefully read her emotions in her eyes.

She touched his face, skimming her fingers across the line of his stubbled jaw.

"You've been clenching your teeth since the moment Trish appeared on the green."

"Have I?" He leaned in closer, inhaling the coconut scent of her shampoo. Why was it that that particular smell was suddenly so incredibly enticing?

"Seth, I...I hope you know you can always count on me. I want to be there for you, whenever and wherever you need me. I know you already finished with the playhouse, and you're doing great with Caden, so there's no reason you need to call on me. But if you want to, I'm offering my friendship, with no obligations attached."

"Whenever?" he repeated, his voice a ragged whisper. "Wherever?"

It wasn't that his problems with Trish and his fears about Caden disappeared, exactly. Rather, they melded with the dozens of other emotions rising to fill his chest. He desperately craved human touch, but not just anyone's.

He wanted to feel that connection with Rachel, and it was unlike any feeling he'd ever before experienced. His chest warmed and his skin tingled as his gaze dropped to her lips.

They'd been through a lot together these past few weeks. He trusted Rachel completely. With her by his side, and aided by prayer, they could face this new challenge.

Together.

"Whenever?" he asked again softly, close to her ear. Her warm breath fanned his cheek. "Wherever?"

At the audible catch in her breath, he slid his arm down around her shoulders.

"How about here? Now?"

He saw the answer in her deep brown eyes, luminescent in the moonlight.

"Thank you," he said, softly brushing his lips over hers. "For being there for me. And for Caden." Each phrase was followed by a kiss, and with each kiss he lingered just a little bit longer on her soft, full lips.

She was oh, so sweet.

Rachel wrapped her arms around his neck and he removed his hat as he slanted his head to deepen the kiss.

He was beyond speaking. He could only feel, not only the gentle press of her lips against his, but all the emotions behind them.

The whiz and pop of fireworks sounded in the distance, but Seth was too absorbed in Rachel, in making fireworks of their own, to even notice the vibrant colors lighting up the sky.

Chapter Nine

The next morning, Rachel awoke to the sound of a lawn mower directly outside her window, the growl of its engine too close to be that of a neighbor's.

She really didn't want to be pulled from her dreams—the ones where she was kissing Seth under the magnificent glow of fireworks.

But when she came fully awake—well, as awake as a person could be before her mandatory two cups of coffee—she realized it wasn't a dream at all.

Seth *had* kissed her last night, and it was one of the most wonderful moments of her life, second only to the first time she'd held Zooey in her arms.

With semiwakefulness also came the doubts and fears, sneaking up on her before she had the ability to keep them at bay.

Yes, Seth had kissed her—but why? Was it the result of true emotions, those that had slowly grown over the time they'd spent together the past few weeks? Her response to him came from exactly that.

But afterward, she realized he could merely have been reacting to the shock of Trish's arrival, needing the feel of one heart connecting to another in order to ground and reassure him, all precipitated by the day's events.

What if his kiss had meant nothing at all?

She couldn't blame him for seeking comfort during such emotional upheaval. It was a very human thing to do. And the truth was, she was more than ready to give him whatever emotional support he needed.

Even if it left her own heart in peril.

She was beginning to care for Seth in a way that went far beyond the solid friendship they had developed, and that put her in a precarious position, totally open and vulnerable to being hurt.

She could very well end up with a broken heart.

She'd had other relationships in the past, but none that compared to what she had with Seth—the bond of friendship that was the foundation of other deeper emotions she'd never experienced before.

But there was so much more to consider than just how *she* felt, even if Seth felt the same way about her.

A relationship with Seth might not even be in *Seth's* best interest. Seth had his hands full to overflowing learning to be Caden's father and a single parent. And a ranch owner.

And now there was Trish.

Even if pursuing a relationship had been a remote possibility before, this would be the worst of all times to do so. Seth needed to keep his head on straight, not be distracted by the staggering emotions a new relationship invariably brought.

Finally, what about Zooey? And Caden? Yes, Zooey had encouraged her to try for this relationship, but she knew her daughter would still be hurt in the end if things went bad. And Caden—that precious toddler had become so much a part of her life that she couldn't imagine no longer being in his world. If they broke up, Seth might even remove him from day care. What then?

She scoffed at herself. She was borrowing a load of trouble where, at least for the moment, there was none.

And there *was* none because there was still time for Rachel to apply the brakes and avoid this potential train wreck altogether.

Whoa, Nellie.

She was shaken from her reverie by an engine cutting out and starting again. Now she was certain there was no doubt about it. There really *was* someone mowing her front yard.

Curious, she peeked out through the curtain and was surprised to find Seth plowing straight, neat rows across her grass, Caden happily strapped in a backpack and enjoying the ride.

What on earth?

Wrapped in a plush cotton robe, she tiptoed up the stairs to see if Zooey had been wakened by the noise, but in typical teenage fashion, the girl was sound asleep.

Rachel took a moment to tuck Zooey's comforter around her shoulders and then she brushed her daughter's hair back and planted a soft kiss on her forehead, just as she used to do when Zooey was around Caden's age.

She quietly closed the door to Zooey's bedroom and returned to her own room to throw on jeans and a T-shirt and run a brush through her bedhead hair.

She didn't think about makeup until she was already out the door and Seth had spotted her. He waved and killed the engine on the lawn mower.

She must look a mess.

Too late now.

Blame it on lack of coffee.

"Why are you mowing my lawn?" she asked bluntly as he jogged up to her.

Again, that lack of coffee...

"Because it needed to be mowed."

"Yes, that's true, but my question is, why are *you* mowing my lawn? It's seven o'clock in the morning on a Saturday. No one gets up at seven o'clock in the morning on a Saturday to mow someone else's lawn."

"I do. I've already eaten a good breakfast and have been for my run. Bright eyed and bushy tailed," he said with a cheesy grin.

"So I see," she said wryly.

"I borrowed your lawn mower out of your shed. I hope you don't mind."

"Why should I mind? Mow away to your heart's content. That's one more thing I can scratch from my list of things to do before the inspector comes."

He nodded. "That's the plan. I know the inspector is coming to evaluate your day care on Monday, so I thought I'd do a little more spiffing up so your place really shines."

Tears sprang to her eyes before her emotions even caught up with her.

"You remembered."

Seth reached up and gently wiped away her tears. "Of course I remembered, sweetheart. If it's important to you, it's important to me."

It was an intimate, caring gesture, made even more so by the kindness in his eyes. Apparently, he was prepared to embrace what had happened between them the evening before and move forward with their relationship.

And she wanted that, too—wanted it so much it terrified her. She'd never been a runner before, but she felt like running. As far and as fast as she could.

She barely stopped herself from scurrying backward. She was an adult and should act like it, but she might as well have been an angst-ridden teenager, as discombobulated as her mind and body were acting.

She wanted to throw away every reason why being with Seth was a bad idea and just *do* it, follow her heart for maybe the first time in her life.

But she would not follow those inclinations, because she couldn't. Because too many people depended on her to keep her head on straight.

"That's so sweet," she told Seth, and meant it with all of her heart.

"I think the inspector is going to be happy with this place, especially when she sees how much your kids adore you."

Rachel laughed. "That will be the one day they all decide to act up. Anyway, it's not the children she'll be examining. She'll be checking off a list of standards every in-home day care in the state must adhere to. Thanks to you and my beautiful new play set, I have high hopes that I'll pass with flying colors."

His hand moved from her face to her fingers, which he squeezed lightly.

"You will. And if for some reason they find something that needs fixing, I'm your man."

I'm your man.

He said it so casually and yet so genuinely, accompanied by a grin that could charm the wrapper off a lollipop, that his words slipped straight through the cracks of the walls she'd so carefully put up and plunged right into her heart.

She might know in her head what was best for all involved, but her wayward heart didn't care to listen to what her mind had to say.

"If you want, I can come over tomorrow and—" Seth started, but he was interrupted by the ring of his cell phone.

He pulled it out of his pocket, checked the number and scowled deeply.

"It's her," he confirmed. "Who would have thought that she was an early riser? I pictured her as the type who stayed up until all hours of the night and then slept until noon."

Rachel had reached pretty much the same conclusions about the woman. She chuckled and nodded toward the still-ringing phone. "Are you planning to answer that?"

"If I ignore her, do you think she'll go away?"

"Doubtful."

He sighed and answered the phone.

"This is Seth...No, you didn't wake me. I was up." He paused as Trish spoke on the other end of the line. "All right. Where do you want to meet?"

Again, a pause. Seth's jaw tightened, and Rachel slid her hand into his free one.

"No, that's probably not going to work. Listen, I have a better idea. There's a café called Cup O' Jo's on the end of Main Street. You probably saw it when you drove in—er, came into town in your limo. You can't miss it. There's a hitching post and water trough out in front of it."

He rolled his eyes and covered the receiver. "She just called Serendipity a hick town," he mouthed.

"Actually, people often ride their horses to the café, so the hitching post gets a lot of use," he informed her.

Rachel covered her mouth so Trish couldn't hear her snickering in the background.

While it was true that Cup O' Jo's occasionally saw a horse hitched to its post, it wasn't exactly a regular occurrence the way Seth was painting it, gently mocking Trish's closed-minded perceptions of the town. Trish probably thought she'd stepped back in time by at least a century.

"All right. I'll see you at two."

Seth hung up and half groaned, half growled from deep in his throat.

"This is one meeting I'm definitely not looking forward to," he said.

"I know. I've been praying for you since the moment Trish showed up yesterday."

"And I appreciate that. It means a lot. But can I ask you for another favor? It's a big one, and I won't blame you if you say no. But I'm really uncomfortable with the idea of meeting Trish alone, even if it's in the middle of Jo's café."

"I don't blame you. She was trying to get you to meet in a private place, wasn't she?"

"As if I'd even consider that."

"That woman has an agenda you know nothing about—and she seems to have a thing for you, too. It's wise to meet her in a public place. Plus, you know Jo will be watching over you, with *your* best interests at heart."

"Right. That was my thought when I suggested the

café. I know Jo will subtly—or not so subtly—keep an ear on the conversation and break in if she thinks she needs to. She's not shy about that. But I would really like it if—" he took a deep breath and plunged on "—if you would agree to come along with me for moral support. I'd feel so much more comfortable with you watching my six."

"If you ask me, I'd better watch your three and nine, too, with that woman."

Seth chuckled, but it was a dry sound nearly devoid of amusement, and Rachel knew why.

Seth was right. Whatever Trish had planned, it would be a lot more difficult for her to accomplish with Rachel sitting at the table with them, even if she didn't say a word.

Ha! As if she would be able to hold her tongue with that woman. If she tried to threaten Seth, or Caden's well-being, Rachel would not be held responsible for what happened after that.

Yes. Rachel had every reason in the world to go—even if she was bolting forward when she'd just this morning once again resolved to pull back.

Just this one time, she promised herself.

Seth needed a friend, someone who understood his situation. She could be that friend for him. She would go with him to meet Trish, and then afterward, if things went well, she'd have to talk to Seth about what had happened on the Fourth of July and how it should never happen again. She wasn't looking forward to that conversation, but she knew it needed to take place.

Or if things went badly, she would wait until an appropriate moment at a later time and offer him whatever kind of support he needed to deal with Trish.

"Of course I'll go," she said, putting a hand on his arm. "You couldn't keep me away."

He visibly relaxed at hearing that.

"Thank you," he said simply, though the words were profound. "Now I'd better finish mowing so we can impress that inspector of yours with your world-class landscaping."

"You mean *your* world-class landscaping."

He grinned. "I say we both take credit for it."

Seth mowed the front and back lawns of Rachel's house, trimmed her bushes and cut back her roses, snipping a few stems to present to Rachel as an impromptu bouquet.

It might have come straight from her own flower bed, but Rachel reacted as if he'd purchased an enormous bouquet of exotic flowers and had it sent by special courier, instead of given her a half-dozen thorn-ridden roses.

"Careful," he said as he transferred the small bouquet into her hands. "These roses aren't the hotbed kind. They have thorns."

"I'm not sorry the roses have thorns," she replied. "I'm just happy that the thorns have roses." She chuckled. "See? You've been rubbing off on me. I'm looking at the bright side of the world instead of dwelling on the overcast."

They'd evidently switched places, because he was seeing clouds all over the place.

"I have a feeling it's going to be difficult to keep a positive attitude today," he admitted. He glanced at his watch. "Speaking of which—I guess it's time for me to face the dragon."

Rachel laughed. "Oh, Seth. You crack me up sometimes. Does that make you Saint George?"

"Don't I wish."

They arrived at Cup O' Jo's about five minutes early, but Seth knew Trish was already there, given the ridiculous-looking stretch limo parked on the other side of the street, taking up practically half a block of parking spaces.

He reached for Rachel's hand and gave it a squeeze as he blew out an unsteady breath.

"Let's do this thing." He straightened his cowboy hat, stretched his neck muscles both ways and tried to relax his shoulders.

Trish was seated in a far corner booth. Her eyes lit up when she spotted Seth, but her lips drooped into a pouty frown when she realized Rachel was with him.

"I thought we were going to meet privately," Trish argued as they approached the table.

"You said that, not me," he said. "Besides, anything you can say to me, you can say to Rachel."

"Why? Is she your fiancée? Your girlfriend?"

The question threw Seth for a moment.

After last night's kiss, he didn't know *what* they were—somewhere in the indefinable space between being close friends and something more. He knew what he wanted them to be, but he wasn't going to go announcing his intentions to Trish before he'd discussed them with Rachel.

"I'm a friend," Rachel said firmly, taking a seat in the booth across from Trish and scooting to the farside so Seth could sit beside her.

A friend?

Was that how she saw him?

"Whatever," said Trish with a dismissive wave. "Seth, it's you I need to speak with."

"About what?" he asked cautiously as Jo set steaming mugs of coffee in front of the three of them.

Trish took one look at the contents of her mug and pushed it aside. "I don't do coffee. Bring me some chai tea."

If Jo was thrown by the woman's rudeness, she didn't show it. She merely picked up the mug Trish had shoved away and smiled at Seth and Rachel.

"Enjoy your coffee," she said with a pert grin.

Trish turned her attention back to Seth. "I'm here to talk about Caden, of course," she said, as if it was obvious.

And it was.

He'd known from the beginning that Caden played into this somehow; he just didn't know the details yet.

But the very thought of Caden being caught in the middle of some tug-of-war made him bristle, even after he'd promised himself he was going to remain calm and composed.

Rachel reached for his hand under the table and linked his fingers with hers.

"What about Caden? Why don't you get right to the point and tell me why you've flown clear across the country to visit a child you've shown absolutely no interest in before this week?"

"Well, he is my nephew," Trish stated, pressing her crossed forearms onto the table and leaning forward. "As his auntie, of course I'm worried about his welfare. He has no one to care for him now."

"He has me."

"Yes, well, that's what my lawyer told me after he

attended the reading of Tracy's will. His understanding was that Tracy and Luke were very specific that Caden's guardianship should go to you."

"Exactly," Rachel said.

Where was this leading? Had Trish really expected to inherit Caden's guardianship after she'd completely alienated her family?

Why would she even want it?

She turned the question on him.

"You're a good-looking single man. Why would you want to be burdened with a baby?"

"Caden is *not* a burden," Seth replied through gritted teeth. Despite his determination to be civil, this woman was really poking at his sore spots.

He didn't like where this conversation was going.

Not at all.

"If you ask me," she said, although no one *had* asked, "it doesn't make any sense at all for you to have him. I mean, let's face it. If you adopt Caden, you'll be a single father. Why would you want to do that to yourself? Forget having any time for yourself. Forget dating. No woman wants a man burdened down with a child."

Trish slid a sidelong glance at Rachel and sniffed, as if she didn't like what she saw.

He didn't know if Rachel was aware of how hard she was squeezing his hand at Trish's scrutiny, but he could tell Trish's words bothered her. He unlaced their fingers and made a big production of putting his arm around her shoulders.

What did Trish know, anyway?

When Seth looked at Rachel, he saw the most beautiful woman in the world—not only on the outside, although in his eyes she was that, but on the inside, because he'd seen her heart.

He'd thought his action would reassure Rachel, but if anything, her shoulders tightened even more and she curled down in the booth.

Trish's expression changed as she narrowed her eyes on the two of them.

"You will also have to ditch other things you probably enjoy, like live sports games," Trish added. "You won't be able to play poker or go out with the boys to hit the bars."

Seth raised his eyebrows.

Wow.

Trish was really shooting in the dark here, trying to guess what he considered to be a priority in his life, and she was missing by miles.

Well, maybe not the live-sports part, but that was a small sacrifice to make for Caden's sake. He could watch his favorite teams on his big-screen television. Not to mention the fact that he had loads of relatives who would be all too happy to take Caden for the day if Seth somehow happened to score some prime tickets.

Even better, it wouldn't be long before he could take his *son* to live games with him—teach him all the ins and outs of every sport. Teach him to throw a football and catch a baseball in his little mitt. Seth could coach Little League. And he would definitely show Caden more parkour moves. The kid was already somersaulting forward and backward like a pro.

Seth was actually excited over the prospect as he saw it, which he expected wasn't the outcome Trish anticipated when she'd made the comment.

Despite his anxiety, he experienced a moment of

true joy. Trish had no idea how much he'd come to love Caden. And that love was going to be what saved the day.

He wasn't going to be a good father.

He was going to be a *great* father.

"You can see where I'm going with this," Trish continued, tapping her fingers on the table.

"No, not really," he said, hoping what he was thinking was wrong.

It just had to be.

"It's just not right for my sister to hand off her kid to a perfect stranger instead of a relative."

"I wasn't a stranger to Tracy. I was very close friends with both her and Luke. In fact, Luke was my closest friend growing up. I was best man at their wedding."

"Maybe that explains their poor decision making," Trish said.

"I'm sorry. What?"

Seth had had enough. At this point, he just wanted to get up and walk away. There was nothing Trish had to say that he wanted to hear.

He was preparing to do just that when Trish spoke again, freezing him in his tracks.

"Let's not bring lawyers into this, okay? I think we're both reasonable adults and can work it out right here between us."

"Work what out?" Rachel asked.

He was glad she spoke, because in his anger, he had completely lost the ability to form words.

"The details," Trish said.

She made a dismissive gesture as if none of that mattered.

"For me to take Caden off your hands."

Chapter Ten

Rachel was worried about Seth. After Trish had made her bold proclamation regarding Caden, which both Rachel and Seth had feared, Seth got up and stomped out of the café, not even bothering to pay for his coffee.

Jo had stopped by their table to ask if everything was all right, but of course it wasn't. Trish didn't care to speak to Rachel, and Rachel couldn't speak for fear of bursting into furious tears.

Jo had graciously said the coffee—and the *tea*, with emphasis—were on the house. Rachel had thanked her. Trish had not.

Rachel had gone searching after Seth, but no one had seen him. He wasn't at the ranch. Samantha was still watching Caden and hadn't heard from Seth at all. Neither had his parents.

Eventually, Rachel returned to her own house and waited, assuming Seth would call or come over when he'd cooled down and was ready to talk.

They had a lot to go over, to work through, in order to eliminate any possibility of Trish making good on her threats to try to take her nephew away. Caden would stay with Seth, if Rachel had to dump her entire life savings into paying a good lawyer to make sure of it.

It was all she could do to pull herself together, but she wanted to appear composed so she could give Seth the support she knew he would need when he sought her out.

Seth was a strong man, but even the strongest men sometimes needed a shoulder to lean on.

She was determined to be that shoulder.

Except he never came.

She'd waited until after midnight to go to bed and woke early for church, hoping he would be there.

He wasn't, and neither were any of the rest of the Howells and Davenports.

Rachel assumed they were with Seth, helping him come up with the best solutions to use to fight against Trish. If she was being honest, it hurt her feelings that Seth hadn't included her in his plan making. After all, she'd been there when he'd met with Trish. She knew better than anyone what he was up against.

But, she told herself every time those thoughts rose, he was with his family, which was where he should be. Those were the people Seth would be counting on to keep Caden safe.

They were Caden's family.

She was just a friend.

When Monday morning came, Rachel had no choice but to switch her thoughts and attention to the upcoming inspection of her day care.

She didn't expect Seth to bring Caden by. Not under the current circumstances. It was understandable that he would want to keep Caden by his side. If the whole family had missed church on Seth and Caden's behalf, she doubted that he'd drop Caden off at a day care and leave him there, even if that day care was hers.

Everything inside the house was spick-and-span and in perfect order, thanks mostly to Zooey, who had offered up her Saturday to do a deep cleaning. Seth had taken care of everything on the outside. Both the front and back lawns and the flower beds were as neat as she had ever seen them. And the new play set was the triumph of them all.

She was nervous, as she always was before an inspection, even though she knew everything was up to standards and she'd done all she could do to see that it went well. She'd been doing in-home day care in this house for long enough that she would have thought she'd be completely confident in the outcome, but there was still that slight little niggling doubt that she had overlooked something important and she would lose her life's work and ability to care for her family.

The day-care kids started trickling in and she set everyone up at the craft table to make puppets out of paper bags. Zooey didn't have summer school on Mondays, so she was crouched at the preschool-sized table, helping the kids cut funny mouths out of colorful construction paper with blunt-edged child safety scissors and paste googly eyes on their projects.

When the doorbell rang at just after ten, Rachel was as ready as she would ever be. She took a deep breath and opened the door.

"Seth," she said in surprise, ushering him and Caden inside. "What are you doing here?"

"Sorry we're late," he said, placing Caden on the floor so he could run and join his friends at the craft table.

"Is everything okay?"

A shot of anxiety passed through Seth's gaze and then it was gone, as quickly as it had come.

"I didn't miss the inspector, did I?"

"No. Actually, when the doorbell rang, I thought it was her."

Rachel's home inspection wasn't what she wanted to talk about, but she respected Seth's unspoken wishes and remained on the topic he had introduced.

"Awesome. I want to be here when she gets her first look at the playhouse."

"Which is no doubt the pièce de résistance of the entire day care. You outdid yourself."

"It was for a worthwhile cause."

"The senior center?" she asked, thinking back to the day of the auction, when Zooey had won the bid on Seth on her behalf.

How much had changed since then. Now she couldn't imagine her life without Seth and Caden in it, even if it was merely in passing when Seth dropped Caden off for day care and picked him up again. At least she'd still be able to spend a big part of her days with that precious little boy who had stolen her heart just as thoroughly as his new daddy.

Which was why it was so crucial that Caden stay with Seth.

Those two special characters had changed her life for the better.

"Not the senior center," Seth said softly, shaking his head. "You."

Her.

Not the senior center. Not even the day care.

Her.

She didn't have time to reflect on what that might mean, because the inspector chose that moment to arrive.

The *she* turned out to be a *he*, and he was very impressed with the work Seth had done on the play set. A weekend hobbyist and do-it-yourselfer, he blatantly admired Seth's skill and workmanship.

The kids came out to play and crawled all over the new equipment. Seth got sidetracked helping a couple of the preschoolers across the monkey bars. The inspector formally approved her day care.

Rachel was relieved that there was one less thing to worry about, but as she called the kids inside for carpet time and out-loud reading time, her mind turned back to the situation of Seth and Caden.

Seth lingered as she read the kids a story and then read the same one again as an encore. The little ones liked the repetition.

She fed them a snack and then it was nap time.

"Coffee?" she asked Seth, who was standing in the middle of the indoor imagination center, pushing a toy truck back and forth with the toe of his boot.

"Sounds good," he whispered, so as not to wake the children.

She gestured toward the kitchen and he followed her inside, where he sat down across from her at the table after she'd served him coffee.

"I was worried about you when you took off that way," she said bluntly. They had only forty-five minutes to talk before nap time was over, and she didn't want to waste even one second on trivialities.

"Yeah. Sorry about that. I needed some time and space to clear my head. But I should have called or texted you or something to let you know I was okay."

His hand curled into a fist around his coffee mug, so tightly that Rachel was afraid the cup might shatter in his grip.

"Where did you go? I checked the ranch and spoke with Samantha and your mother. No one knew where you were."

"I went to one of my mom and dad's cabins. They didn't even know I was there until the next day. Samantha took care of Caden for me."

He paused and swept in a breath.

"I was so angry and was feeling so panicked that I was afraid I might frighten Caden if I picked him up from Samantha's in that state. I don't ever want Caden to feel like Daddy's angry."

"It happens. Everyone needs to step back and cool off sometimes."

"What happened after I left? Sorry I stuck you with the check."

"You didn't miss much. Jo stopped by the table and absolved us of our bill. Trish didn't have the least interest in speaking to me, so she took off right after you did. I stayed and ate a piece of Phoebe's famous pie."

"Apple?" One side of his mouth kicked up.

"Cherry." She raised her hand and waved it. "Guilty. Emotional eater here."

"Nothing wrong with pie."

For one beat the tension lightened, but then it came crackling back and they both instantly sobered.

"Have you heard any more from Trish?"

He shook his head. "No, but I don't know whether I should be relieved or worried that she hasn't tried to contact me."

"Maybe she changed her mind," Rachel said hopefully, even though she knew better.

"Or else she's revving up to go full-court press on me."

Rachel deduced that it was a sports reference, but she didn't know which sport. Not that it mattered. She understood the gist of it.

"I've been thinking and praying about this ever since we met with her," Rachel said.

"Yeah. Me, too. I've been kicking thoughts around with my family, but we haven't come up with much."

"I have a few ideas," she ventured.

"I thought about calling you, but frankly, I didn't want you there."

"Oh." She was confused and hurt and felt like he'd just stabbed her in the heart with a steak knife.

"Look. I was ashamed of myself. I didn't want you to see me after I'd acted that way."

"What way?"

"Angry. Frustrated. Panicking. It was bad enough having to have my family there to see me all unwound, and they've known me their whole lives."

"I guess I understand where you're coming from, but I want you to know there is no possible condition I could see you in that would change my perception of you," she said, putting her whole heart into her words.

"That's what my mom said. My sister, too. They said I didn't put enough confidence in you, that you were a stronger woman than I gave you credit for. They told me I was stupid for walking out of that café without you. And I guess I was."

It was silly, but she was beyond relieved that he'd shut her out because of his focus on maintaining her positive image of him and not because of anything she'd done—although that nonsense had to stop right now.

So Seth was human. He got angry. Didn't everyone?

He was being far too hard on himself. He had good reason to be upset. Trish had managed to rattle the status quo in his life, and he had every right to be thrown by it.

Even Rachel felt as though she were precariously balancing on a precipice.

"Did you come up with any good ideas? What do you plan to say to Trish when you see her?"

"That I'm getting a lawyer, I suppose, despite Trish saying she doesn't want to go that direction. I put in a call to the lawyer who executed Luke and Tracy's will, but he hasn't gotten back to me yet."

"I've been thinking about it also, and I'm not sure you're going to need a lawyer to fix this problem."

"Why? Just because Trish said not to bring them in? I'm going to need all the backup I can get."

"That much is true. But as far as Trish saying she doesn't want lawyers involved—I think she's showing her hand. A lot of her story doesn't add up. Her not getting her lawyer involved is just the start of it—a major clue."

"How so?"

"Don't you think it's odd that she wants to challenge the will but doesn't want to bring lawyers into this? She's pressuring you into thinking that giving Caden to her would be the best thing for you, giving you all these silly reasons that don't make any sense. And yet she expects you'll just hand the baby over to her and be done with it. I think she doesn't want you going to lawyers because she knows she doesn't have a legal case. She's hoping you'll just decide to give him up."

"That's not going to happen."

"No. And we'll fight to keep Caden to our last penny if necessary. But think about it. If she believed she had a legal foot to stand on, don't you think she'd have brought her lawyer front and center? She has the money and the resources, obviously. Why come herself?"

"I don't know."

"Me neither. I can't think of a single rational reason. It seems to me to be the move of a desperate woman."

"A *crazy* woman," Seth agreed.

Rachel brushed a lock of hair off her shoulder.

"She didn't even go to her sister's funeral, never mind the reading of the will. She sent her *lawyer* to represent her. It was completely impersonal. And now she's going face-to-face with you, trying to act like the loving auntie, implying that she'd be a better parent for Caden. Do you see where I'm going with this?"

"Keep talking."

"I think her lawyer came back from verifying Luke and Tracy's will and told her she *had* no real inheritance. I think she feels ripped off—upset that Caden got everything and she got nothing."

"It's true. Caden was the major beneficiary of the will, which makes perfect sense, since he's their only son. I'm sure Tracy left her sister some keepsakes or something."

"No doubt. But I don't think keepsakes are what Trish is after."

"You think she's after cash?"

"It makes sense, doesn't it? She clearly doesn't care

for Caden, so she's after something else, something she thinks Caden can give her."

Seth scoffed and shook his head. "But it's not like Caden's inheritance is a big stash of money sitting in a bank. They had a little in savings and a college fund they'd started for Caden, but everything else Luke and Tracy had was wrapped up in the land. I can't imagine Trish being any more interested in cattle than she is in toddlers."

"I don't think she's interested in the land, unless she wants to liquidate it."

"Which she can't do. The land is in trust as Caden's legacy. As his guardian, I'm supposed to keep the ranch running for his benefit. I couldn't sell it if I wanted to, not without permission from the trustee."

"Good. That's one less reason she has to pursue this madhouse scheme. Honestly, I don't even think she's given a thought to the ranch."

One corner of Seth's lip quirked in amusement. "No, I am guessing not."

"Is there any way she'd be able to get her hands on Caden's college fund?"

"Absolutely not. No one can touch that money until Caden is old enough to attend college. Not even me. That's all done by a trustee at the bank." He shook his head. "But I still don't get it. Why would she come out here thinking to take Caden for the money? Raising a child is a huge responsibility, not to mention a money drain. I can't imagine why Trish would really want to take him on. And why would she need to if it's money she's after? She seems to already have more money than she knows what to do with. I'm no connoisseur on such things, but it looks to me like she dresses in some pretty fancy, high-priced clothes. And she rode into town in a stretch limo, for crying out loud. She's got to be loaded."

"Maybe," Rachel agreed. "But looks can be deceiving. She's clearly desperate, and if it has nothing to do with Caden's well-being, then it almost has to be about money. She hasn't thought this all the way through, because I can't imagine her wanting to be saddled with a baby, even to get her hands on his trust fund. Maybe she just wants to make a point and then threaten you into giving her what she wants without the baby changing hands."

"What she wants? You mean like a bribe?"

"I don't know. Maybe. I can't think of any reason why she would make the effort to fly across the country and try to settle with you on her own other than something to do with the almighty dollar. It could be that the rich just want to get richer, although it's strange that she'd go to all this trouble if she's already loaded."

"Wow. You really have thought it through. One thing I admire about you—you have a special sense about people. You're empathetic. I think you may have hit the nail on the head about Trish coming out here trying to wrest Caden's trust fund from him."

"If that's the case, then she's following a dead-end trail and she doesn't even know it," Rachel pointed out. "What we have to do now is make her realize that on her own. I don't think talking to her is going to be good enough to get it through that thick head of hers, especially when she thinks she has a bargaining chip in being Caden's blood aunt."

He clicked his tongue against his teeth and chuckled.

"Why do I have the feeling you've already got an idea formed in that wonderful, brilliant mind of yours?"

"I might," she said, teasing him. "But I have to prepare snacks before I get the kids up from their naps and things are going to get kind of hectic from this point on. Do you think we could meet with your family tonight, say about seven o'clock, at your folks' lodge? I'll explain my plan in detail then and we can get everyone's take on it. If I'm right, Trish may decide to turn tail and head back to the big city on her own."

"And good riddance. But you're not going to give me any hints?"

She smiled mischievously. "Not a one."

"Fine. Dangle the carrot and then make me wait. That's cruel and unusual punishment, you know."

She laughed and bobbed her eyebrows. "It'll be worth the wait, I promise you."

"I believe you, sweetheart. I'll see you tonight."

Seth paced back and forth across the polished oak hardwood floor in the main lodge of his parents' bed-and-breakfast, eager for the family meeting to start.

He'd teased Rachel about dangling a carrot, and it had seemed funny at the time, but now it was driving him stir-crazy knowing she had an idea about how to keep Trish from taking Caden away but not knowing what it was.

It was raining cats and dogs outside, but, ignoring both the storm and the mud that caked to his shoes, he'd already taken a long run down one of the nearby trails.

Twice.

Will and Samantha and the children were playing a board game in one corner of the guest lobby, while his parents puttered around with the never-ending projects that made their bed-and-breakfast such a big hit in the local area and beyond.

He was debating setting off on a third run when Rachel appeared at the door, wiping her feet on the mat before removing her rain boots and folding her umbrella.

"Finally," he said, rushing up to her and taking her by the elbow. "My mom has snacks set up at their kitchen table. Everyone is anxious to hear what you have in mind."

And by *everyone*, he meant himself.

Rachel chuckled and pulled back. "At least let me take off my raincoat first."

He assisted her, gentleman that he was, and hung the coat on the rack, then ushered her into the kitchen, where the rest of the adults gathered, leaving the kids to play together.

"As you all know, we've been dialoguing on the situation with Trish," Seth said by way of opening. "In short, we both see clues that lead us to believe she isn't quite who she says she is."

"She's not really Caden's aunt?" Will asked, his eyes widening in surprise. "I thought that was a given."

"No, no. She's unquestionably Tracy's sister," Seth said.

"When we met with her," Rachel said, jumping in before the conversation went offtrack, "she tried several different tacks to persuade Seth that he didn't really want the responsibility of Caden's guardianship and that he should simply hand Caden over to her."

"Which I told her in no uncertain terms was never going to happen. I wouldn't give Caden up for anything."

"Not even the chance to go see more live sports

games, which truly is impressive," Rachel teased, winking at Seth. His family laughed.

"She made all of these really lame arguments in favor of me retaining my bachelor status," Seth explained, "but I shut her down, at least at first."

"And then came a really strange stipulation," Rachel said, picking up the thread again. "She expected that Seth would buy into her arguments about Caden and that he'd want to hand over his guardianship of the boy, but she didn't want to get any lawyers involved."

"Well, that's ridiculous," said Samuel, shaking his head. "Impossible. Seth is Caden's legal guardian. Even if he wanted to, he couldn't just pass Caden off to her like a football."

"Which I don't," Seth grumbled.

Amanda put her hand on Seth's shoulder. "We know you love Caden, son. You don't have to keep reminding us."

"I know. I just get riled up every time I think about some of the things that woman said."

"Back to the lawyers?" Samantha suggested.

"It seemed an odd request for Trish to make," Rachel continued. "If she thought she could contest the will through the court system and win, she would have sent along one of her high-priced lawyers. I'm guessing the lawyer she sent to the reading of Tracy's will has already told her that Caden's guardianship is securely locked up in Seth."

"Which is why she flew across the country to do this herself." Seth scoffed. "I believe she honestly thought, at least at first, that I could be easily talked out of caring for Caden."

Samantha snorted. "As if that woman has any interest at all in Caden's well-being."

"None of us believe that she does," said Amanda.

Rachel nodded. "So Seth and I asked ourselves—if her interest doesn't really lie with Caden, then why is she here?"

"The answer is money," Seth said. "We think she wants to try to claim Caden's inheritance."

"Preposterous," Samuel said with a huff of breath.

"Why would she need money?" Samantha asked. "Her purse alone is worth more than I make in a month at the grocery store."

"This is the part we're a little iffy on," Rachel admitted. "All we can do at this point is make an educated guess. Maybe it's just a grudge, because she thinks the will was unfair? In her view, she got nothing from Tracy, and Caden got everything."

"Of course he got everything," Amanda said, appalled. "He's their son."

"Obviously, we don't know what her financial situation is like," Rachel said. "It could be that she's just greedy and wants everything for herself. It could also be that she's not as well-to-do as she would have everyone believe."

"We all know that Caden's inheritance is tied up in Hollister ranch land," Seth said. "I'm pretty sure she doesn't want to have anything to do with cows. And if she's looking at Caden's trust fund, she'll have to look elsewhere, because that money belongs to him. No one can touch it. Not even his guardian."

"So basically what you're saying is she's going on a wild-goose chase," Samuel said. "Taking on Caden's guardianship is a financial liability."

"Not to me," said Seth. "But to her? Yeah."

"So—you think if she is in possession of the full picture, she won't try to take Caden from you?" Amanda asked.

"It might take a little more coercing than that," Rachel suggested. "I'm not sure simply talking to Trish is going to do any good. But I thought maybe if we *showed* her, she might be less inclined to pursue this current line of reasoning."

"And now Rachel is going to tell us how we are going to do that," Seth said, hoping she truly had a solution up her sleeve. Because he agreed with her that talking to Trish would get them nowhere.

"I say we give her a little taste of what her future would look like should she take over Caden's guardianship. There's a little risk involved, but I think it's our best play."

"This isn't a Hail Mary, is it?" Seth said, his throat closing around his breath.

He didn't even *like* the word *risk*. Not when Caden was involved.

"I don't know what that is, but I'm guessing you're not talking about a prayer, are you?"

Samantha laughed. "Leave it to my baby brother to couch his sentences in football terms."

Rachel smiled and shrugged. "Sorry, not my game."

Seth rolled his eyes. "Rachel doesn't have a game."

"But she has *game*, which is far more important, right, Rachel?"

"I should think so," Rachel said. "Now, what's a Hail Mary?"

"Sometimes in the last few seconds of play, if a team is losing but could potentially win with a touchdown and they are too far downfield to execute a normal play, then the quarterback—that's the guy who throws the ball—throws it as hard and as far as he can and hopes that one of his receivers can get upfield fast enough to catch the ball and make a touchdown," Seth explained. "Needless to say, that doesn't work very often."

"So you're asking if my plan is basically a shot in the dark?" Rachel competently condensed his drawn-out explanation.

Samantha laughed. "That's the short version. I like yours better."

"Can something go wrong? Maybe. But I don't think we're looking at a wing and a prayer. We don't actually have what Trish wants. At the end of the day, Trish can't take something we're legally unable to give her. She won't listen if we try to explain it to her, but if we show her what she would really be signing up for, I don't think she'll be so quick to pick up that pen. More than likely, she'll scurry back to where she came from."

"How are we going to show her?" Seth asked, interested but not thoroughly convinced.

If it could happen, if they could make Trish go away, he could look forward to his future—a future with his custody of Caden secure...and hopefully Rachel by his side. It would be a whole new world for all of them, and he wouldn't take it for granted. He would thank God every day for all His blessings.

Rachel grinned, and Seth thought he might have seen a bit of a puckish gleam in her eyes.

"I'm glad you asked. That is where you all come in. We have to think of ways to help her visualize what her life might be like if she were to take over Caden's guardianship. If we make it real enough to her, she won't be coming back, even with a lawyer."

She pulled open the notebook she'd brought with her and clicked on the pen.

"Put your thinking caps on, ladies and gentlemen, and let's get creative."

Chapter Eleven

Rachel couldn't help but laugh as she surreptitiously watched Trish pick her way across the dirt to Seth's office at the Hollister ranch. The limo had had to stop halfway down the driveway or risk getting permanently stuck in the mud, so Trish had to make it the rest of the way on foot.

In heels.

Spiky ones.

At least the woman was predictable.

Trish scrunched up her face in disgust as she carefully dodged the many cow pies littering the area. Rachel suspected her distress was as much from the pungent smell as it was from trying not to land an expensive shoe in a pile of pucky.

Someone *may* have let ten head of cattle onto that ground earlier in the day, and Seth certainly hadn't had time to remove the droppings.

No—he was too busy riding the range and herding cows. He wasn't going to have time to shower, so he was bound to come in dusty and smelling of horse.

The copy of the legal document outlining the terms

of Caden's trust—twenty pages of legalese on a blue background—was propped neatly on the desk, waiting for Trish's perusal.

Most important of all, Caden was sitting on Zooey's lap on a blanket in one corner, quietly playing with a set of toy cars.

Everything was in place.

Now it was up to Trish to show her hand and admit to the real reason she was here.

Rachel glanced once again at Caden and Zooey, so sweetly interacting together. Her heart clenched in her throat when she considered that this evening might be the last time they were together like this.

After tonight, when they'd effectively banished Trish from Seth and Caden's life, Rachel and Seth would have no more reasons to seek each other out. She wasn't even sure Seth would keep Caden in her day care once she was finally able to speak with him.

Was she crazy, talking herself out of the opportunity to be in a relationship with the best man she'd ever known?

The man she was in love with?

The answer was an unquestionable yes, and though her heart was breaking into terribly painful shards, it was best for everyone to end things now—before their lives got more complicated.

But oh, how it hurt.

As it was, Zooey had already bonded with Caden in a special way, and he clearly adored her. That alone was reason enough to be steadfast in her decision. A failed relationship would be far too damaging for everyone involved, not just Rachel and Seth.

She couldn't go there. She couldn't risk hurting the children.

"Oh, it's you," Trish said when she walked in the door and slammed it behind her with an annoyed huff of breath. "When Seth asked me to meet him in his office, I assumed he meant a nice professional building—not some run-down add-on in the middle of a *barn*."

"Come on in, Trish, and make yourself at home," Rachel said with a smile. "You'll find this place is quite cozy. Seth runs all of the Bar H ranch business from here. If you're serious about taking up Caden's guardianship, you'll be spending quite a lot of time here."

"But it smells." Trish cupped her palm over her nose and mouth. "Like cows."

"Yes, that's generally the primary aroma on a cattle ranch, although you'll probably get a nice whiff of horses, pigs and chickens as well, when you take a full tour of the place. Don't worry—you'll get used to it."

"What do you mean, *I'll* get used to it?"

On cue, Seth stepped through the door. Rachel almost cheered at how he had outdone himself. She was honestly impressed. She didn't know what he'd done to make himself look quite so…dirty. It looked rather as if he'd rolled in the pigsty.

Maybe he had. He smelled bad enough, and there were streaks of mud on both cheeks and all down the front of him. If he'd wrestled with the pigs, he'd lost.

But to Rachel, he had never looked better.

What was wrong with her?

Trish gaped as Seth flashed her his most charming grin and then removed his hat and slapped it against his thigh. Clouds of dust burst forth and then slowly settled on the ground at his feet.

"Long day riding," he said by way of apology. "Do you know how to ride a horse, Trish?"

She shook her head violently. "I haven't been on horseback since I was a child. The closest I've ever been to a horse in twenty years is a carriage ride through Central Park."

"Oh, well, no matter. I was out of practice when I started, too. It's easy enough to pick back up if you put some real effort into it."

"What are you talking about?" she demanded.

Seth raised a brow. "I thought Rachel would have told you. The Bar H ranch comes with Caden. They're a package deal."

She looked alarmed for a moment and then nodded as an idea hit her. Rachel knew exactly what she was thinking. She could almost see the dollar signs in Trish's eyes.

"Okay. I can live with that. How much money do you think I can make selling it off? Do you know someone who might want to commercialize the land, or am I better off trying to sell it as is?"

"Yeah, well, that's just it," Seth said smugly, and then paused for dramatic effect.

Rachel didn't know if Trish was holding her breath, but Rachel was, just waiting for the punch line.

"You can't sell the ranch."

"What?" Trish squeaked. "I thought you just said the ranch comes with Caden."

"Oh, it does. It's his legacy, written into the will, which you would know if you had been at Tracy's funeral. You can't sell the ranch. If you take over Caden's custody, then you have to see that the ranch prospers for the next twenty years so Caden can take it over when he reaches manhood."

Trish grabbed the nearest chair and sat down. Rachel could tell the wheels in her brain were spinning, trying to make this new piece of information work into her plan.

"It's hard, physical work, but it's quite fulfilling, I assure you," Seth continued. "I never thought I'd want to be a cowboy, but actually, it kind of fits my style."

And it did, more even than Seth probably recognized.

"I am not leaving New York City to come live on a ranch," Trish protested. "I was born on a ranch and I promised myself I would never go back."

"Hmm," said Rachel. "That's unfortunate. I mean, you can talk to Wes, the ranch manager, but there are a lot of day-to-day decisions that will have to be made by you. I don't think you can do that long-distance—at least not if you want the ranch to thrive, for Caden's sake."

"She means make money," Seth clarified.

Trish already looked overwhelmed.

Now for part two.

"I assumed you'd want to look at the paperwork for Caden's trust fund."

Rachel scooped it off the desk and handed it to Trish. The type was so small Rachel couldn't even make it out with her reading glasses on. Not that it would have mattered. She didn't understand half of what the paper said anyway, and she doubted Trish would be able to, either.

Trish scanned the paperwork with a frown, but her eyes lit up when she spotted the figure with the dollar sign and several zeroes after it.

"That's the value of all the assets being held in trust,

including the dollar value for the ranch," Seth pointed out. "There's some cash in savings, true, but it's for his college education," Seth explained before Trish exploded with joy.

"But he'll be getting the ranch. A cowboy doesn't need a college education."

"And there's where you're wrong," Seth said, leaning his hip against the desk and crossing his arms. "A ranch owner needs a good business education. I've just signed up to start taking online business classes on the GI Bill. Trust me, there is much more to cattle ranching than herding stock from pasture to pasture. Accounting, for one. How are you with numbers?"

He winked at Rachel. She was still trying to absorb the new information Seth had just shared. She had no idea he'd signed up for an online college. She was proud of him for his foresight. He'd really embraced his role as guardian of the ranch as well as little Caden.

He'd taken the curveballs that life had thrown him and used them—not to give up on his dreams, but to alter them into something better.

Just as she'd had to do when she was sixteen, pregnant and alone.

Trish set the legal papers back on the desk—upside down, as if she didn't want to look at them.

"It doesn't matter," she said. "Caden is two. He won't be in college for years. I can borrow the money and then pay it back when it's time for him to go to school."

"Actually, you can't," Seth said smoothly.

"And why not? It would be my—er, Caden's—money."

"*Just* Caden's money," Rachel replied. "Locked in until he turns eighteen and earning good interest."

"*Locked* in?" Tracy sounded appalled—and a little discouraged.

"The trust fund is run by a trustee from the bank. Not even Caden's guardian, whoever that might be, can touch it."

"So there's no money there, either."

Trish was thinking hard. Rachel could tell their plan was working. Now all that was left to cinch the deal was the grand finale.

Caden.

This was the part of the plan Seth was most nervous about. Everything else had gone off without a hitch. He was pretty sure Trish was doubting herself right now—trying to figure out how she was going to come out on the winning side of things and starting to realize there *was* no winning side. Or rather, no way to win if you wanted just the benefits without the responsibilities. Responsibilities that had frightened Seth at first, but that he was now happy to embrace. He was starting to feel at home in his role as rancher, and he loved being Caden's daddy. His heart ached at even the thought of giving that up.

But whether he liked it or not, Caden was the crux of this entire matter. They had given Trish a lot to think about. Hopefully, she had seen by now that trying to get guardianship of Caden was a losing proposition—

Not in *her* best interest.

And there was one way to prove it.

He met Rachel's eyes and she nodded briefly.

It was time.

He walked over to the corner and gently lifted his son into his arms, giving him a soft, reassuring kiss on the cheek before turning to Trish and carefully settling the toddler in her lap.

She sat frozen to the spot, stiff and unyielding. She didn't try to engage with Caden. Trish looked like she thought if she moved, Caden might bite.

Fortunately for her, Caden wasn't a biter.

Much.

Seth took a deep breath and plunged in, even though his gut was churning and he wanted to snatch his son back out of that woman's arms.

"If you really want guardianship of Caden, I imagine you'll want to get to know him better."

"I...er...yes, okay," she said, looking around nervously at anything but Caden.

"I'm sure you've thought a lot about how you'll take care of him. It will take careful management of the ranch to continue to make a real profit. You'll probably have to invest your own money into covering your expenses. What is it you said you do in New York?"

Trish didn't answer. She'd clasped her hands around Caden and was rubbing them together, one over the other.

"Well, you'll have to focus on learning ranching for now," Seth said. "It's a full-time job, so you'll want to find a decent day-care provider for Caden. You'll be in the area, so I recommend Rachel here. She runs the best day care in the county. No—that's not right. In all of Texas."

"My facility is just a small home-run operation. I'm sure you'll want him in one of those high-end preschools," Rachel added. "Pretty pricey, and it's going to be a long commute each way, but entirely worth it if you want all the bells and whistles the top-tier preschools offer—foreign-language lessons, musical training, the works. Caden is a smart kid. He's already showing potential in several areas. I'm very impressed by his early learning skills."

Trish looked as if she were choking.

"Were you thinking of a private school?" Seth asked. "He'll need to be in a heavily academic school if he wants to get into an Ivy League college. Oh—and you'll want to make sure he plays sports. Whatever interests him."

Not that Seth felt that there was any need to send Caden to an Ivy League school, unless that was what he wanted. There were plenty of good colleges and universities out there, and the important thing was getting a solid education that would prepare Caden for the life he wanted to lead. Maybe an expensive private school would have the best program for that—maybe not. It would be Caden's decision, either way.

But with her designer-label lifestyle, Trish seemed the type to assume more expensive automatically meant better. Even if that involved pulling Caden from Rachel's day care, where he was loved and appreciated, and dumping him into some high-pressure day care that crammed the kids full to bursting with education and discipline but probably skimped on individual care, affection and fun.

"And since the money for his education can't be touched until he's ready for college, that means the tuition costs before that will have to come from you."

He couldn't believe he was saying this—talking about Trish's role in Caden's upbringing as if it were really going to happen. As if there were even the slightest possibility that he would hand off his guardianship to this woman.

He wouldn't. Not in a million years.

No worries, he reminded himself. They were talking her *out* of guardianship, not into it.

And it was working.

"Aside from school," Rachel said, "children are a persistent drain on your bank account. Clothes, food, diapers. Although obviously, you don't have to worry about money."

Rachel had phrased the sentence as a given, but in truth, Seth knew she was trying to ferret out the real answer.

And Trish was turning green. And red. And purple.

A whole rainbow of colors.

"I don't have any money," she mumbled, almost too low to hear.

"I'm sorry, what was that?" Rachel asked.

"That's why I came here. I work as a fashion buyer's assistant. I planned to go to school, but that never worked out. I'm a glorified secretary. I don't make much money, and living in New York is expensive."

Now that Trish had started talking, the whole story poured out of her.

"I was too ashamed to go to Tracy's funeral and let everyone see what a failure I am, so I sent a lawyer. I really had to scrape to put that together. I thought I'd get some kind of inheritance that would allow me to finally go to school. But when the lawyer came back, he said all of Luke and Tracy's money was tied up in Caden's trust."

"Meaning land," Seth said.

"Yes," Trish agreed with a rueful chuckle. "I got that message loud and clear."

Telling her story was apparently cathartic to her. As she relaxed, so did Caden, so much so that he fell asleep in her arms. She stroked his silky hair, the first time she had really touched him.

"He is a sweetheart, isn't he?" Trish murmured.

"Yeah," Seth said, his voice cracking with emotion. "He is."

Trish sighed. "Obviously, I didn't think this thing all the way through. I wasn't going to neglect him," she assured them. "I just had this vague notion that once I got Caden's guardianship, I wouldn't have to worry about money. I was going to get a live-in nanny. I know nothing about children. I thought I could raise him without really interacting with him."

She paused and sighed again. "But now I realize what a mistake that would have been. I was thinking about what I wanted—not what Caden requires or deserves. Caden needs love and attention, and that's what you two give him."

Seth's heart warmed toward Trish. And he didn't try to correct her about his relationship with Rachel. They might not be officially in a relationship yet, but he intended to fix that as soon as possible.

"Believe it or not, I was raised in a very close-knit family," Trish continued. "Tracy and I were best friends. She loved the ranch, but my passion was sewing and designing clothes. I got it in my head that I was going to take off and make a big-name label for myself." She scoffed. "Not so much, huh?"

"But what about your clothes? The limo?" Rachel asked, her voice now gentle and empathetic.

Trish's eyes filled with tears. "I wanted you all to think I was a big success so giving me Caden's guardianship would seem like the right thing to do. The clothes were easy—I have access to a lot of samples through my work. As for the rest...in reality, I've maxed out my credit cards. I've got nothing left."

"Then send the limo away," Seth said. If someone had told him two hours ago that he would be feeling compassion for Trish, he would have laughed in that person's face. But now—

"I know Serendipity is not New York, but we've got a strong community here that will help you get back on your feet. You can stay in one of my parents' cabins until you get settled."

Her eyes brightened for a moment, but then hope once again faded. Seth knew the feeling of saying goodbye to your dreams. But he also knew the blessing of embracing new ones.

Better ones.

"Let me talk with my best friend, Lizzie," Rachel added. "Her family owns Emerson's Hardware. I think maybe we can find a position for you there."

"You want me to work in a *hardware store*?" Trish asked, surprised. "I know even less about hardware than I do about ranching."

Rachel laughed. "Emerson's is a catchall in a town as small as this. If you want clothing, you go to Emerson's. It's all Western wear, but I imagine they'd be open to suggestions on how to spruce up their offerings. They may even take to the idea of you producing your own line, if you can come up with something that fits the style around here."

For the first time since he'd met her, Trish was glowing with enthusiasm. Her expression turned the hard, obnoxious woman into a real live human being. Who knew that under all that brass was a person who was hurting, who was secretly waiting for someone to reach out to her with kindness?

"You would do that for me? After the way I treated you?" A tear slipped down her cheek.

Rachel laid a hand on her shoulder. "Absolutely. We'll help you however we can to get you back on your feet."

"And another benefit of staying right here in Serendipity is that you'll be able to see your nephew whenever you want and really get to know him," Seth added.

Trish smiled softly, a real, genuine smile, then sniffled and tried to wipe her tears with her shoulder.

"You'd better take Caden," she told Rachel. "I don't want him to get soaked when I start bawling."

"So you'll stay?" Seth asked as Rachel settled Caden on the blanket in the corner, where Zooey was lying on her back. The teenager smiled and slipped earphones into her ears before cuddling with the toddler.

"No hard feelings?" she pressed.

"None," he assured her. "Now, if you'd like, I'll help you get settled with my parents for tonight. You can send for your suitcases tomorrow."

Seth was gone for maybe half an hour, and he was anxious to get back to Rachel, who'd stayed behind to watch the kids.

"I can't believe how great this all worked out," he announced as he entered the office. "Can you believe after all the kerfuffle that Trish was just a mixed-up woman in need of help? I'm so relieved that I'm shaking. This is awesome."

Rachel held a finger to her lips.

"Shh. The kids are both sleeping. Zooey's just as conked out as Caden is. I thought she was just listening to her music until I heard her snore."

He grinned. "They look good together, don't they? Like brother and sister?"

Rachel gasped.

He reached for her waist and turned her around to face him, but she didn't quite meet his gaze. He put a finger under her chin and tipped her head up until their eyes met.

"What? What's wrong?"

He'd thought he'd be coming back to celebrate, to whirl her around and kiss her silly. As far as he was concerned, the night couldn't have turned out any better.

His *life* couldn't be any better. But—

"Rachel, talk to me."

"We can't do this, Seth. You know we can't."

He frowned, his eyebrows lowering. His gut tightened until it hurt. He didn't want to hear what was coming next, but he had to ask.

"Do what?"

"Be together. You. Me. We've got to stop this now, while we're still able to."

He didn't know about her, but he was well past being able to stop his emotions. He was flat-out in love with her.

"What if I don't want to stop?"

She laid her forehead against his shoulder and groaned softly.

"You're not making this easy. I don't want to stop, either. I...I...care for you. Very deeply. But it's not just about us."

Her coconut shampoo assaulted his senses as he

pulled her close. He wanted to kiss her until she realized that there was no way for them to be apart.

He didn't want to live his life without her. He loved her. Caden loved her. Caden already looked up to Zooey like a sister, and he suspected Zooey wouldn't object to the news that her mom and Seth were a couple.

She pulled in a breath and leaned back. This time, she looked him straight in the eye.

"Say we did get together, start a real relationship. What if we break up? Zooey and Caden have grown so close to each other over the past few weeks. And she thinks *you* hung the moon."

She pulled in a raspy breath. "So what happens when we are no longer together? It won't just be our lives that are ripped apart, but theirs. I can't risk doing that to Zooey, or to Caden. I just can't. You've got to understand, Seth."

He tensed and let go of her, afraid he'd hold her too tight. Because he never wanted to let her go. He wouldn't prevent her from walking away if that was what she was determined to do—but he was nowhere near done trying to convince her to stay.

"No, I don't have to understand. You've already got us breaking up when what I see is a wonderful future in front of us. What about that, Rachel? What if we could be happy together? If you're going to take a risk, why not risk that, huh?"

"I'm sorry," she said, her voice cracking with strain. "I've thought this through and I've made up my mind."

She'd hit him right where it hurt.

His heart.

"So that's it, then. We stop seeing each other?"

"We can still be friends."

"Friends. Right. Like that ever happens."

"It could."

Seth couldn't let it go. He couldn't let *her* go. But he saw no way to convince her, unless—

"Okay, then. I agree. Friends. But as a *friend*," he said, emphasizing the word, "I would like to invite you and Zooey to my parents' place for Caden's third birthday party two weeks from Saturday. I think he would be really upset if you missed it."

"I wouldn't think of it."

"Of going?" He was so frustrated he wanted to run for miles. Just not away from her.

"No. Of missing it. Zooey and I will be there. What time is the party?"

"Three o'clock."

She leaned over to shake Zooey awake. The teen stumbled to her feet, muttering something about hard floors.

"Three o'clock it is, then," Rachel said, starting to walk past him. "Good night."

He reached for her elbow and gently pulled her back to him, brushing his lips over her cheek.

"Good night, Rachel."

She didn't respond to his kiss but just kept walking. Out the door, and apparently, right out of his life.

Chapter Twelve

The day of Caden's birthday arrived, sunny and warm, the perfect day for an outdoor party at the Howells' bed-and-breakfast. The whole family would be there, and Seth had invited Trish—all information that Rachel had obtained from Trish herself. She and Trish had spoken several times over the week and were fast becoming friends.

But as far as *other* friends went, Rachel wasn't talking to Seth at all. Samantha had been dropping Caden off at day care, and though she was friendly with Rachel, they never spoke of Seth. She hadn't seen him since that night in the office, and she wasn't certain she was prepared to see him today.

If he looked at her the way he had that night in the office—the love in his eyes, followed by pain and confusion—she didn't know if she could stand it.

Friends.

They could be friends.

She just had to buck up and stuff all her emotions somewhere deep inside, where they wouldn't interfere with Caden's birthday celebration.

Zooey had come down early, for Zooey. A typical teenager, she usually slept past noon on a Saturday. But this Saturday was important to her. She hadn't quite hit coming downstairs early enough for breakfast time, but they had an early lunch before they wrapped Caden's gifts and headed off to the bed-and-breakfast.

Rachel dragged her feet, forgetting this and that and remembering something else she had to do, until she had completely annoyed Zooey.

"Mom, you're always on time," Zooey complained.

"On time is late," Rachel quipped.

"Then why is it three fifteen and we still haven't left the house? What's up?"

Rachel shook her head. Her daughter was far too perceptive. She was going to have to play this carefully.

"I'm just a little scatterbrained today."

Zooey shot her a look that told her she didn't buy it, but she didn't push the subject, thankfully.

They were the last to arrive at the party. Rachel recognized most of the kids toddling around as children from her day care. Trish was helping Amanda bring out dishes piled with food. They were chatting amicably, and Trish looked the best she had since she'd arrived in Serendipity—heavy makeup washed off, fashionable clothes put aside for jeans and a colorful top, frowning displeasure replaced with a bright smile, like a load had been taken off her shoulders.

Rachel supposed it had, although it would still be a steady climb for Trish to get back on her feet.

Now it was Rachel with the load on her shoulders, but she wouldn't let anyone see that.

Not on Caden's birthday.

Rachel laughed when Zooey caught sight of Dawson.

Apparently, he had a little sister who'd been invited to the party and he was the chaperone. It wasn't long before he wandered over and started talking to Zooey. Rachel was glad Zooey wasn't the only teenager at the event, but seeing her daughter so happy with Dawson made her heart ache.

Rachel had never known young love, and the only real love she'd ever had—

She cut that thought off without finishing it.

Seth was playing horseshoes with Samuel and didn't notice she'd arrived, or else he simply didn't acknowledge her.

Which was fine.

She sat down at a picnic table where Will and Samantha were in a heated match of cribbage. Rachel was content just to watch the interplay between the married couple, but envy sneaked up on her. The green monster was really on her heels today.

Soon it was time for cake and the birthday song. They took pictures while Caden grabbed a fistful of chocolate cake with white icing and smashed it on his face, mostly missing his mouth.

Rachel's heart welled with affection for the little boy. They'd been through so much together that Rachel didn't think that special place in her heart reserved for Caden would ever go away.

But then again, neither would that Seth-sized hole.

Her heart must look like Swiss cheese.

After cake came presents. Zooey was super excited for Caden to open her present, a stick horse that made neighing sounds when he pushed its ear. Caden loved it, and after all the gifts were unwrapped, he charged off to play cowboys and cowgirls with his friends.

The adults pulled out a board game and nearly everyone joined in—Trish, Amanda and Samuel and a few parents who were chaperoning their children at the party. Even Dawson and Zooey participated.

Pretty much everyone was there except Seth, who had disappeared.

He hadn't spoken to her once since she'd arrived at the party, and she was respecting his space. He was probably angry with her for the way she'd left things, and she couldn't blame him for that.

But someone had needed to say the words. She hated that it had had to be her.

Soon she was caught up in the game, belting out answers and receiving a marker for each right guess. The first person to get six markers won the game.

Rachel wasn't particularly competitive, but it kept her mind off Seth, so she threw herself into the game, and before she knew it, she had five markers and her next turn had arrived.

Samantha was reading off the question on the card.

"This one's for the win," Samantha reminded everyone. "Okay, Rachel, are you ready?"

Rachel laughed and nodded.

"The topic is sports."

She groaned. "Well, I'm not winning this turn. I know zilch about sports."

Samantha grinned. "Don't be so sure about that. Now here we go. In the game of football, what is it called when a quarterback launches the ball upfield during the last seconds of the game in the hope of a touchdown?"

"Are you kidding me right now?" Rachel asked.

"No. Seriously. That's the question. I read it word for word. And I know you know the answer to it."

"Unbelievable. The one and only sports question I can answer. It's called a Hail Mary."

The adults around the table clapped, and Zooey hooted.

"Way to go, Mom!"

"Aaaand she's in for the win," Samantha announced excitedly. "Way to go, sis."

Wait, what?

Had Samantha just called her *sis*?

"Thank you for ruining the surprise for me," came Seth's smooth tenor voice from behind her.

She stood up from the picnic table so fast that she bumped her elbow. Seth reached out to steady her.

"That had to hurt. Are you okay? Do you need a bandage with a cartoon on it and someone to kiss your owie better? I'm getting pretty good at that."

Rachel laughed, although she'd never been so confused in her life.

"I think I'll live."

"Good to know," said Seth. "Because I kind of want you around. For a long time. Like the rest of my life."

Rachel had lost her voice. This was nothing like what they'd decided together that night at the office. He was looking at her with such love in his eyes that there was no possible way anyone in the vicinity could miss it.

What had happened to being just friends?

"I thought a lot about what you said the other night. About being friends. About not wanting to hurt anyone, especially the children. And you are right about that."

She leaned forward to whisper in his ear. "Is this really a conversation we should be having in front of other people—especially your family?"

He chuckled. "I should think so. I want everyone to hear what I'm about to tell you."

He reached into the pocket of his red chambray shirt and retrieved a small black velvet box.

Rachel's breath caught in her throat and for the life of her she couldn't dislodge it. And her heart—

Her heart was swelling until it hurt.

"Like I said, I've been thinking about the talk we had. And I realized what part of the equation was missing." He grinned. "I solved for X."

He went down on one knee and opened the velvet box to display a beautiful square diamond solitaire with tiny diamonds lining it all around. It was the most beautiful ring she'd ever seen, from the most wonderful man she'd ever known.

"I love you, and I think I have for some time now, but I realized after talking to you that love is not enough. I want you to be able to see the future with me and Caden and believe in it. You've had people leave you behind before, and I understand that you're scared it might happen again. But I am pledging my permanent commitment to you, and to the kids, before God and all these witnesses. I promise to guard your heart always. Zooey and Caden will have a stable home with two parents who love them—and each other."

He stopped and cleared his emotion-clogged throat. "Because I do love you, Rachel. So much. Will you be my wife?"

Tears flowed freely down Rachel's face as she reached out her hand. Seth stood and placed the ring on her left finger. He framed her face in his hands and smiled down at her.

"God was answering our prayers when we weren't

even looking," he murmured huskily. "I love you, Rachel, with my whole heart."

"And I love you." Those were the only words she could manage, but she knew the rest of what she wanted to say was in her eyes.

His lips came down on hers just as the applause started. She vaguely heard the hooting and hollering.

"Way to go, *new sis*."

"Welcome to the family."

"Yay, Mom. I knew he was the right guy for you. I told you so."

Seth kissed her until she couldn't breathe and then he kissed her some more. Her head was spinning by the time he lifted his lips from hers, and that was only enough for him to whisper one word close to her ear.

"Awesomesauce."

* * * * *

Don't miss these other heartwarming stories about surprise babies leading to lasting love in the COWBOY COUNTRY *miniseries:*

YULETIDE BABY
THE COWBOY'S FOREVER FAMILY
THE COWBOY'S SURPRISE BABY
THE COWBOY'S TWINS
MISTLETOE DADDY

Find more great reads at www.LoveInspired.com

Dear Reader,

Are you ready for the story of another bachelor from Serendipity's First Annual Bachelors and Baskets Auction benefiting the senior center? If you've been reading my books for long, you know how crazy things can get when the community gets together, and Seth and Rachel are no exception.

Rachel has already experienced raising a child as a single parent, while for Seth, it's brand-new when he suddenly becomes the guardian of two-year-old Caden. It may seem like these two are at completely different places in their lives, but when they get together, they discover that two families are better than one.

I'm always delighted to hear from you, dear readers, and I love to connect socially. You can find my website at www.debkastnerbooks.com. Come join me on Facebook at www.Facebook.com/debkastnerbooks, and you can catch me on Twitter under the name @debkastner.

Please know that I pray for each and every one of you daily.

Love Courageously,
Deb Kastner

COMING NEXT MONTH FROM
Love Inspired®

Available July 18, 2017

A GROOM FOR RUBY
The Amish Matchmaker • by Emma Miller

Joseph Brenneman is instantly smitten when Ruby Plank stumbles—literally—into his arms. The shy mason sees all the wonderful things she offers the world. But with his mother insisting Ruby isn't good enough, and Ruby keeping a devastating secret, could they ever have a happily-ever-after?

SECOND CHANCE RANCHER
Bluebonnet Springs • by Brenda Minton

Returning to Bluebonnet Springs, Lucy Palermo is determined to reclaim her family ranch and take care of her younger sister. What she never expected was rancher neighbor Dane Scott and his adorable daughter—or that their friendship would have her dreaming of staying in their lives forever.

THE SOLDIER'S SECRET CHILD
Rescue River • by Lee Tobin McClain

Widow Lacey McPherson is ready to embrace the single life—until boy-next-door Vito D'Angelo returns with a foster son in tow. Now she's housing two guests and falling for the ex-soldier. But will the secret he's keeping ruin any chance at a future together?

REUNITING HIS FAMILY
by Jean C. Gordon

Released from prison after a wrongful charge, widowed dad Rhys Maddox wants nothing more than custody of his two sons. Yet volunteering at their former social worker Renee Delacroix's outreach program could give him a chance at more: creating a family.

TEXAS DADDY
Lone Star Legacy • by Jolene Navarro

Adrian De La Cruz is happy to see childhood crush Nikki Bergmann back in town and bonding with his daughter. But he quickly sees the danger of spending time together. With Nikki set on leaving Clear Water, could their wish for a wife and mother ever become reality?

THEIR RANCH REUNION
Rocky Mountain Heroes • by Mindy Obenhaus

Former high school sweethearts Andrew Stephens and Carly Wagner reunite when Andrew's late grandmother leaves them her house. At odds on what to do with the property, when a fire at Carly's inn forces the single mom and her daughter to move in, they begin to agree on one thing: they're meant to be together.

LOOK FOR THESE AND OTHER LOVE INSPIRED BOOKS WHEREVER BOOKS ARE SOLD, INCLUDING MOST BOOKSTORES, SUPERMARKETS, DISCOUNT STORES AND DRUGSTORES.

Get 2 Free Books, Plus 2 Free Gifts—
just for trying the Reader Service!

Love Inspired

YES! Please send me 2 FREE Love Inspired® Romance novels and my 2 FREE mystery gifts (gifts are worth about $10 retail). After receiving them, if I don't wish to receive any more books, I can return the shipping statement marked "cancel." If I don't cancel, I will receive 6 brand-new novels every month and be billed just $5.24 for the regular-print edition or $5.74 each for the larger-print edition in the U.S., or $5.74 each for the regular-print edition or $6.24 each for the larger-print edition in Canada. That's a saving of at least 13% off the cover price. It's quite a bargain! Shipping and handling is just 50¢ per book in the U.S. and 75¢ per book in Canada.* I understand that accepting the 2 free books and gifts places me under no obligation to buy anything. I can always return a shipment and cancel at any time. The free books and gifts are mine to keep no matter what I decide.

Please check one:
☐ Love Inspired Romance Regular-Print
(105/305 IDN GLWW)

☐ Love Inspired Romance Larger-Print
(122/322 IDN GLWW)

Name _____ (PLEASE PRINT) _____

Address _____ Apt. # _____

City _____ State/Province _____ Zip/Postal Code _____

Signature (if under 18, a parent or guardian must sign)

Mail to the **Reader Service:**
IN U.S.A.: P.O. Box 1341, Buffalo, NY 14240-8531
IN CANADA: P.O. Box 603, Fort Erie, Ontario L2A 5X3

Want to try two free books from another line?
Call 1-800-873-8635 today or visit www.ReaderService.com.

*Terms and prices subject to change without notice. Prices do not include applicable taxes. Sales tax applicable in N.Y. Canadian residents will be charged applicable taxes. Offer not valid in Quebec. This offer is limited to one order per household. Books received may not be as shown. Not valid for current subscribers to Love Inspired Romance books. All orders subject to approval. Credit or debit balances in a customer's account(s) may be offset by any other outstanding balance owed by or to the customer. Please allow 4 to 6 weeks for delivery. Offer available while quantities last.

Your Privacy—The Reader Service is committed to protecting your privacy. Our Privacy Policy is available online at www.ReaderService.com or upon request from the Reader Service.

We make a portion of our mailing list available to reputable third parties that offer products we believe may interest you. If you prefer that we not exchange your name with third parties, or if you wish to clarify or modify your communication preferences, please visit us at www.ReaderService.com/consumerschoice or write to us at Reader Service Preference Service, P.O. Box 9062, Buffalo, NY 14240-9062. Include your complete name and address.

LI17R2

SPECIAL EXCERPT FROM

Love Inspired

Ruby Plank comes to Seven Poplars to find a husband and soon literally stumbles into the arms of Joseph Brenneman. But will a secret threaten to keep them apart?

Read on for a sneak preview of
A GROOM FOR RUBY *by* **Emma Miller,**
available August 2017 from Love Inspired!

A young woman lay stretched out on a blanket, apparently lost in a book. But the most startling thing to Joseph was her hair. The woman's hair wasn't pinned up under a *kapp* or covered with a scarf. It rippled in a thick, shimmering mane down the back of her neck and over her shoulders nearly to her waist.

Joseph's mouth gaped. He clutched the bouquet of flowers so tightly between his hands that he distinctly heard several stems snap. He swallowed, unable to stop staring at her beautiful hair. It was brown, but brown in so many shades...tawny and russet, the color of shiny acorns in winter and the hue of ripe wheat. He'd intruded on a private moment, seen what he shouldn't. He should turn and walk away. But he couldn't.

"Hello," he stammered. "I'm sorry, I was looking for—"

"*Ach!*" The young woman rose on one elbow and twisted to face him. It was Ruby. Her eyes widened in surprise. "Joseph?"

"*Ya.* It's me."

Ruby sat up, dropping her paperback onto the blanket, pulling her knees up and tucking her feet under her skirt. "I was drying my hair," she said. "I washed it. I still had mud in it from last night."

Joseph grimaced. "Sorry."

"Everyone else went to Byler's store." She blushed. "But I stayed home. To wash my hair. What must you think of me without my *kapp*?"

She had a merry laugh, Joseph thought, a laugh as beautiful as she was. She was regarding him with definite interest. Her eyes were the shade of cinnamon splashed with swirls of chocolate. His mouth went dry.

She smiled encouragingly.

A dozen thoughts tumbled in his mind, but nothing seemed like the right thing to say. "I…I never know what to say to pretty girls," he admitted as he tore his gaze away from hers. "You must think I'm thickheaded." He shuffled his feet. "I'll come back another time when—"

"Who are those flowers for?" Ruby asked. "Did you bring them for Sara?"

"*Ne*, not Sara." Joseph's face grew hot. He tried to say, "I brought them for you," but again the words stuck in his throat. Dumbly, he held them out to her. It took every ounce of his courage not to turn and run.

Don't miss
A GROOM FOR RUBY
by Emma Miller, available August 2017 wherever
Love Inspired® books and ebooks are sold.

www.LoveInspired.com

Copyright © 2017 by Emma Miller

Reward the book lover in you!

Earn points from all your Harlequin book purchases from wherever you shop.

Turn your points into *FREE BOOKS* of your choice
OR
EXCLUSIVE GIFTS from your favorite authors or series.

Join for FREE today at
www.HarlequinMyRewards.com.

Harlequin My Rewards is a free program (no fees) without any commitments or obligations.

MYR17